DATE: 39:09:26

SERIAL NUMBER: 8834991-X

ITEM:
The Imperial Handbook: A Commander's Guide

DESCRIPTION:
Small printed volume with black cover

FILED BY: Commander Luke Skywalker,
Alliance Command

This copy of the Imperial Handbook dates from just before the destruction of the first Death Star at the Battle of Yavin. The Imperial military stopped distributing these immediately afterward, so finding one in good shape is rare.

The information in here could be vital to the war effort, now that the Empire is on the defensive after our win at Endor. This volume reveals the composition and organization of the Imperial Army, Navy, and Stormtrooper Corps, plus a surprising amount of detail concerning experimental technology and superweapons.

We've pulled in some top officers to give their thoughts, including General Carlist Rieekan of Alliance Command, Imperial defector General Crix Madine, Commander Wedge Antilles of Rogue Squadron, Alliance Commander-in-Chief Mon Mothma, and even Han and Leia. I can't wait to start.

IMPERIAL
HANDBOOK

A COMMANDER'S GUIDE

PART III: THE IMPERIAL ARMY

PART IV: THE STORMTROOPER CORPS

PART V: THE IMPERIAL DOCTRINE

A CONCLUDING NOTE FROM HIS IMPERIAL MAJESTY

INTRODUCTION

By His Imperial Majesty, Emperor Palpatine

The Empire has existed for nineteen years but stands poised to reign for a thousand more. The shift from a Republic to an Empire represents a transfer of power unprecedented in the history of the galaxy. But the Republic could not continue and its people were desperate. When the assembled politicians of the Republic refused to choose between success and ruin, I made the choice for them.

We have achieved glory in unification. Under the Empire we celebrate:

> » ONE RULER
> » ONE CODE OF LAW
> » ONE COMMON TONGUE
> » ONE EDUCATION IN SOCIAL PROGRESS

And the Empire has no tolerance for those who would disrupt this unity. Violence must be met with violence. It is the only language understood by rebels and traitors.

As a commander in my service, you are part of the largest fighting force in the history of the galaxy. Learn your place—and do your duty.

Emperor Palpatine

His Imperial Majesty, Emperor Palpatine

PART I

THE IMPERIAL MILITARY

By Admiral Wullf Yularen

The Empire is vast, and our agents are everywhere. Through this, we demoralize our foes. Through this, we inspire our loyalists.

The scale of the Imperial war machine is unprecedented. Never before in the history of the galaxy has such a fighting force been assembled. Never in such numbers, never with so much variety, and never on so many worlds. There is little in the galaxy that is not under the Empire's control, and it is but a trivial act for the Empire to annex a new world when the Emperor wills it.

That does not mean our challenges are non-existent. It is easy for citizens to slip into indolence and sloth, and from there be swayed into criminality or treason. The Imperial military is ever present to remind citizens of the consequences they face if they stray. Those who are loyal find great comfort in the Imperial military, who ensure alien barbarians will never run wild over the cities of their home planets.

This manual is issued to you, an officer in the Emperor's service, so you may grasp the scope of your responsibilities and the honor bestowed upon your rank.

"UNDER THE EMPIRE'S NEW ORDER, OUR MOST CHERISHED BELIEFS WILL BE SAFEGUARDED. WE WILL DEFEND OUR IDEALS BY FORCE OF ARMS. WE WILL GIVE NO GROUND TO OUR ENEMIES AND WILL STAND TOGETHER AGAINST ATTACKS FROM WITHIN AND WITHOUT. LET THE ENEMIES OF THE EMPIRE TAKE HEED: THOSE WHO CHALLENGE IMPERIAL RESOLVE WILL BE CRUSHED."

—FROM THE TEXT OF EMPEROR PALPATINE'S INAUGURAL SPEECH, DELIVERED 16:5:24

I sat in the Senate chamber when Palpatine delivered these silver lies. The applause of my colleagues was the worst part. —Mothma

THE EMPIRE'S NEW ORDER

—OUR PATH TO VICTORY—

The blueprint for Emperor Palpatine's rule is called the New Order. It is a fitting name for a system that has jettisoned the impracticalities and clutter of the Old Republic.

The New Order is a direct response to the Old Republic's failures, and a wise correction to its excesses. Under the New Order, failed "everyone is right" democracies have been replaced by a clear structure—one that is both authoritarian and militaristic. Its tenets are upheld by the Commission for the Preservation of the New Order (COMPNOR). The benefits of such a structure include:

» **CENTRALIZED AUTHORITY.** There is no question of who is in charge, and it eliminates grandstanding careerism among senators.

» **AN OVERWHELMING MILITARY.** If danger threatens the Empire, from within or without, our armed forces respond with swift, merciless retribution.

» **A RELIANCE ON WHAT IS REQUIRED, NOT WHAT IS DESIRED.** Bare essentials are the core of efficiency. Imperial framework is reduced to its essence, revealing function through form.

» **CORE-CENTRIC POLITICAL RULE.** This is a necessary concession, as the alien species of the Rim are notoriously unpredictable and given to violent outbursts. The history of the Republic Senate is proof that primitives are not fit to hold court in our institutions, or even to govern their homeworlds. By assuming direct control over Rim affairs, we are doing these populations a great mercy. In extreme cases, it has been necessary to orchestrate strategic extinctions in the interest of galactic security.

» **NATIONALIZATION OF COMMERCE.** The Empire approves of corporate competition, and even established the Corporate Sector where transparent mercantilism could occur without interference. Nevertheless, no company should line its coffers at the expense of the greater good. The Empire has nationalized many longstanding corporations, including TaggeCo, Kuat Drive Yards, and Santhe/Sienar, allowing their

Instead they replaced it with grandstanding careerism among moffs and admirals. —Leia

This is no exaggeration. I saw it from the inside. —MADINE

Chewie and me aren't welcome back in the Corporate Sector. I think we squeezed all the money out of that place. —Han

engineers to contribute to our collective prosperity.

» CULTURAL DOMINANCE.

The Commission for the Preservation of the New Order recognizes that authority is more than dominance of the battlefield—it is also dominance of the *mind*. COMPNOR's Coalition for Progress monitors artistic works to ensure they show proper veneration toward His Imperial Majesty. <u>Artists who exhibit subversive tendencies are provided the necessary reeducation.</u>

» BY OUR OWN HANDS.

The Jedi Order is in the past. No longer will proud humans suffer under the elitist rule of an aberrant bloodline. Their tricks have been revealed for the shams they always were. If the Jedi had any true power, would they have been cut down so easily by clone troopers? Lord Darth Vader and other high-ranking acolytes are rumored to possess illusion-making skills similar to the Jedi, but they have pledged to employ them in full cooperation with the Emperor's wishes. Any who don't are to be exterminated.

The Imperial subjects want nothing more than peace. The New Order is a welcome change for those for whom the ravages of the Clone Wars are a fresh memory.

As a commander in the Imperial military, you are an influential figure. Through your actions you will inspire recruits to join the academy, increase the number of COMPNOR enrollees, and persuade citizens to take responsibility for their neighbors' actions and report them. All this will prove valuable when the Imperial military is called to bring the <u>hammer of justice down on a Rebel hotbed.</u>

LOYALTY MUST BE CHALLENGED. IMPERIAL SUBJECTS SHOULD NEVER BE COMFORTABLE WITH PASSIVITY.

HISTORY OF THE GALACTIC EMPIRE

—OUR GLORIOUS FUTURE—

It has been less than two decades since our Emperor first issued his Declaration of a New Order. While some recruits have only dim memories of the previous era (or no memories at all), many of us can recall the shocking excesses that made Palpatine's proclamation inevitable.

Even today, you will encounter some who argue that the Republic could have been saved through reforms and corrections. Those who say this are fools.

The Republic lay in its own waste for millennia. "Give the system time to work!" was the cry I heard time and again. A thousand years is enough to establish whether a system is viable, Senator.

If a patient has been injected with slow-acting poison, a surgeon will cut off the limb before it reaches the heart. Emperor Palpatine possessed similar wisdom. His speech before the Senate struck some as arrogant, but their opposition gave the New Order its first list of enemies.

Those who had stood against Supreme Chancellor Palpatine during the Clone Wars found they had placed a losing bet. Where are they now? If you have a strong stomach, check the Imperial Execution Logs.

Militarization is the cure for the disease the Old Republic wrought upon the galaxy. The New Order provides that salvation through the Imperial Navy, Army, and Stormtrooper Corps.

"BY BRINGING ALL THE GALAXY UNDER ONE LAW, ONE LANGUAGE, AND THE ENLIGHTENED GUIDANCE OF ONE INDIVIDUAL, THE CORRUPTION THAT PLAGUED THE REPUBLIC IN ITS LATER YEARS WILL NEVER TAKE ROOT. REGIONAL GOVERNORS WILL ELIMINATE THE BUREAUCRACY THAT ALLOWED THE SEPARATIST MOVEMENT TO GROW UNCHECKED. A STRONG AND GROWING MILITARY WILL ENSURE THE RULE OF LAW."

—FROM THE TEXT OF EMPEROR PALPATINE'S INAUGURAL SPEECH, DELIVERED 16:5:24

STRUCTURE OF THE IMPERIAL MILITARY

—AN UNSHAKABLE FOUNDATION—

Any machine can be understood by examining its parts. The Imperial military is no different.

The military ultimately answers to our commander-in-chief, Emperor Palpatine, but our highest organizational body is the Imperial High Command. This committee oversees Naval Command, Army Command, Stormtrooper Command, and all support branches.

Regardless of the threat, the Imperial High Command must coordinate the proper combination of ground, air, space, and special ops forces to achieve the mission objective. Imperial High Command also synchronizes our military efforts with those of Imperial Intelligence, COMPNOR, and other intergovernmental partners.

The Imperial High Command has authority over the following military branches and divisions:

IMPERIAL NAVY

The Empire's spacefaring force embodies Imperial power through its Star Destroyers and other mighty warships, as well as the ubiquitous squadrons of TIE starfighters (see detailed analysis in Part II).

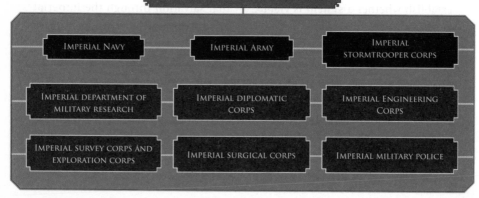

STRUCTURE LEADS TO EFFICIENCY, EFFICIENCY LEADS TO ORDER.
REMEMBER YOU ULTIMATELY SERVE THE EMPEROR.

IMPERIAL ARMY

The Empire's planetary invasion and occupying force is known for its AT-AT walkers and heavy assault vehicles in addition to the courage of its front-line soldiers (see detailed analysis in Part III).

Imperial Stormtrooper Corps The Empire's first-strike force, with their distinctive white armor, operates in hazardous environments across the galaxy (see detailed analysis in Part IV).

IMPERIAL DEPARTMENT OF MILITARY RESEARCH

The Empire's weapons research division manages numerous top-secret projects that have resulted in astounding new warships, armaments, and battle stations (see detailed analysis in Part V).

IMPERIAL DIPLOMATIC CORPS

The Empire's diplomacy branch is an oft-overlooked but necessary function when dealing with hostile worlds. The ambassadors and negotiators attached to the Diplomatic Corps ensure that occupied populations adhere to the Emperor's dictates, reducing the need for pacification by force.

IMPERIAL ENGINEERING CORPS

The Empire's engineering branch is tasked with constructing garrisons and other structures of strategic value, including ore mines, power generators, and space stations.

IMPERIAL SURVEY CORPS AND EXPLORATION CORPS

The Empire's mapping and exploration divisions are attached to the Imperial Navy. These frontier scouts help expand the Empire's borders by identifying worlds primed for conquest or exploitation.

IMPERIAL SURGICAL CORPS

The Empire's medical branch operates in surgical theaters and aboard naval warships near planetary battlefields. Their knowledge has been used to develop new methods of biological warfare.

IMPERIAL MILITARY POLICE

The Empire's internal military police force keeps order within the ranks as needed, though our troops are so well-disciplined that such action is rarely required.

I know a bartender on Commenor who'd disagree. —Han

Notoriously corrupt, every one of them. Their willingness to take bribes has been a huge asset for the rebels. —Leia

HOW CAN WE MANAGE A GALAXY?

—OUR STRATEGIC VISION—

Planetary governance under the New Order flows top-down, from the central authority. The Imperial military maintains order to keep the Empire prosperous and secure. As you will see, we are taking steps to make this hierarchy even more efficient.

DISSOLUTION OF THE IMPERIAL SENATE

The Imperial Senate will no longer exist by the time you read these words. It served as a transitional buffer between the Old Republic and the New Order, but it has outlived its usefulness.

By cutting the last ties to the past, the Emperor will banish the failed philosophy of representation by majority. Instead of senators, Imperial subjects will now have the benefit of sector governors to administer to their needs.

For too long, the Senate has been a refuge for the defiant. Those opposed to the Emperor's rule fancy themselves noble idealists, and their puffery has come dangerously close to treason. They will no longer have an official outlet for their lies.

Imperial Intelligence reports that some members of the Senate have even begun collaborating with the Rebel Alliance. They have been identified and will be dealt with.

You will see public communications stating that the suspension of the Senate will last "the duration of the emergency only." But know the Emperor's decision is final.

I had "disappeared" before the dissolution occurred. I could serve Chandrila far better from there.
—Mothma

"THE NEW ORDER OF PEACE HAS TRIUMPHED OVER THE SHADOWY SECRECY OF SHAMEFUL MAGICIANS. THE DIRECTION OF OUR COURSE IS CLEAR. I WILL LEAD THE EMPIRE TO GLORIES BEYOND IMAGINING."

—FROM THE TEXT OF EMPEROR PALPATINE'S INAUGURAL SPEECH, DELIVERED 16:5:24

REDISTRICTING OF IMPERIAL TERRITORY RESULTS IN INCREASED EFFICIENCY

Our new Oversectors are comprised of many smaller sectors. This structure allows for direct command of military forces, control of information, and more efficient taxation of Imperial subjects.

A regional governor, or Grand Moff, commands each Oversector. A sector governor, or Moff, administrates each smaller sector. The governors have direct political and military control over their territories.

As a military commander, this structure is your greatest asset. Politicians will now back your actions. You will not be pulled in competing directions for the chain of command is clear. You are free to enforce the Empire's will through strength of arms.

PROPAGANDA: CONTROLLING THE NARRATIVE

The Commission for the Preservation of the New Order (COMPNOR) organizes institutional and public support for His Imperial Majesty and the precepts of the New Order.

Membership in COMPNOR is popular among loyalists, for it is the most visible way to demonstrate faithfulness to our ideology. Through COMPNOR's cultural and youth groups, the Empire can control the story and the reactions of its subjects. The volunteer patriots of COMPNOR keep watch on their neighbors and inform us of suspected collaborators. COMPNOR also operates its own paramilitary unit, CompForce.

The media NewsNets are no longer private entities. Imperial HoloVision is now the official outlet for public consumption of current events. Other, unofficial entities, such as *TriNebulon News*, *Brentaal Trade News*, and *Core News Digest*, understand that publishing a story or spreading any disloyal sentiment is punishable.

BECAUSE THE EMPIRE CONTROLS THE MEDIA, WE CAN TURN ANY NEWS TO THE EMPEROR'S ADVANTAGE.

This will be a problem if we hope to capture the Core worlds. We need to get our own story out there. —MADINE

SPIES AND SECRET POLICE

—OUR INVISIBLE SOLDIERS—

The advanced work and findings collected by Imperial Intelligence and the Imperial Security Bureau are vital before a battle can be launched. These agencies are the central intelligence services for the Empire.

Spies can be just as valuable as soldiers with the information they can gather on the strength and composition of enemy forces. However, the notorious Bothan Spynet is not under Imperial control. We suspect they are in league with the Rebel Alliance.

NOT ALL OF THEM. BUT ENOUGH. —RHEEKAN

IMPERIAL INTELLIGENCE STAYS AWAY FROM THE FRONT LINES, BUT EVERY DECISION MADE BY A COMMANDER IS INFORMED BY THEIR FINDINGS.

IMPERIAL INTELLIGENCE

At the close of the Clone Wars, the agency known as Republic Intelligence was restructured into Imperial Intelligence. The agency gathers information through passive and active surveillance. Its covert agents infiltrate planetary governments and criminal syndicates, including the Hutt cartels and the Rebel Alliance.

It is overseen by the Ubiqtorate, a secret board answerable to the Emperor and the highest echelons of Imperial Command. The only acknowledged member of the Ubiqtorate is the Director of Imperial Intelligence, who serves as the public face of the agency while concealing the full scope of the agency's operations.

Divisions of Imperial Intelligence include:

ANALYSIS: This group processes staggering amounts of data pulled in every second from every world in the Empire. Among this division are the following sections:

» Media: Examines the NewsNets to search for negative sentiment and hidden meanings

» Signal: Monitors carrier waves, image packs, and more to locate valuable information disguised as line noise

» Cryptanalysis: Breaks codes and ciphers *ARTOO COULD OUTPERFORM THE WHOLE DIVISION, I BET.* **—LUKE**

» Tech: Reverse-engineers hardware to develop new listening and recording devices

» Interrogation: Draws information from enemy agents through one-on-one questioning

INTELLIGENCE: This division takes the data from Analysis and uses it to predict movements of the Empire's enemies.

» Sedition: Flags any group with the potential for organized resistance

» External Communications (ExComm): Relays highly secure messages between Intelligence and the military

BUREAU OF OPERATIONS: Being the core of the agency, this group oversees six subdivisions of critical importance:

» Surveillance: Identifies suspects for observation and follow-up

» Renik (Counter-Intelligence): Uncovers enemy infiltrators within our own command structure

» Diplomatic Service: Handles treaties, annexations, and other political missions

» Infiltration: Dispatches highly trained agents for deep cover operations

» Destabilization (Destab): Unbalances local governments, making military conquests far easier

» Assassination: Eliminates targets with quiet efficiency

IMPERIAL COMPLINK: This group scans communications across holonet and subspace, intercepting data and flagging troublesome words or phrases.

SECTOR PLEXUS: Charged with storing all data collected by Imperial Intelligence, this group manages the largest database in existence, dwarfing the digital library of Obroa-skai.

INTERNAL ORGANIZATION BUREAU: This internal-affairs division ensures the loyalty and incorruptibility of all agents and personnel.

ADJUSTMENTS: These black-ops agents report directly to the Ubiqtorate. They are called in as a last resort when other operatives fail. They have substantial resources at their disposal, including experimental gear developed by the Imperial Department of Military Research.

INQUISITORIUS: The Inquisitors are the Emperor's shadowy agents. They are among those whom the Emperor calls his Dark Side Adepts. Chief among their duties is to hunt, capture, and interrogate Jedi. Some of the Inquisitors may even be former Jedi themselves. While classified as part of Imperial Intelligence, the Inquisitorius division reports directly to Emperor Palpatine.

IMPERIAL SECURITY BUREAU

The Imperial Security Bureau operates in parallel with Imperial Intelligence and many of its functions overlap with those of its "older brother." Yet the

The Inquisitors receive surprisingly little mention in this manual. Was the Emperor keeping them a secret due to their Force powers? The military mind doesn't trust it, and would rather deny it. —LUKE

NOT THIS MILITARY MIND. THE ALLIANCE IS GLAD TO HAVE SKYWALKER ABOARD, AND ANY OTHERS LIKE HIM. —RIEEKAN

ISB is a recent organization, founded under the auspices of the New Order. It exists to ensure ideological consistency within the Empire's internal operations. The agents of the ISB are essentially the Empire's secret police.

Branches of the ISB include:

SURVEILLANCE: Tasked with uncovering disloyalty and inefficiency, this branch reports all infractions directly to the central ISB hub on Coruscant.

INVESTIGATIONS: An interagency group that coordinates with the Imperial military to undergo infiltration and undercover surveillance.

INTERNAL AFFAIRS: This division has broad-ranging authority to police all Imperial agencies including science, commerce, and Imperial law.

REEDUCATION: This source of propaganda implements forcible training in the precepts of COMPNOR for those convicted of disloyalty.

ENFORCEMENT: A paramilitary force that provides the muscle needed to ensure other divisions of the ISB have the means to carry out their directives.

INTERROGATION: The agents assigned to question captured subjects for information (with a much higher success rate than the interrogators of Imperial Intelligence). It's what they don't say that's so chilling.
—Leia

IMPERIAL INTERROGATORS ARE RUTHLESSLY EFFECTIVE, ABLE TO EXTRACT A CONFESSION FROM ALMOST ANY PRISONER.

IMPERIAL POLICIES

—ZERO AMBIGUITY—

As a commander, you must be versed in the standard Imperial procedures for dealing with fringe groups.

BOUNTY HUNTERS

The Bounty Hunters Guild is now an Imperial-allied holding, thanks to an understanding between Guild Leader Cradossk and the Empire's law enforcement division. If "the highest bid makes the rules," as the bounty hunters believe, the Empire's treasury should easily pay for the capture or assassination of our most notorious enemies.

PIRATES AND PRIVATEERS

While these groups are similar, privateers are ostensibly in our camp. They have received a letter of marque by Emperor Palpatine entitling them to raid enemy shipping on his behalf. If you encounter an Imperially licensed privateer in the Outer Rim, give them freedom to operate if it doesn't interfere with your own affairs.

Pirates do not operate under the Empire's authority. The sentence for piracy is death.

The "incident"? We kicked their tails! —Han

SMUGGLERS

The incident at Nar Shaddaa is fresh in our memories, and reports indicate that these outlaw couriers are not to be underestimated. Most smugglers are employed by the Hutt cartels. While the Empire does not tolerate lawlessness, the Hutts are important players in the Outer Rim's economy. Any aggressive actions to shut down the smuggling trade should first be cleared with Imperial Command.

ALIENS

While always troublesome, many alien populations on the Rim are primitive and of little threat. However, be careful not to ignore them, or you may be forced to put down an unexpected native uprising. Obedient populations may be needed by the Imperial Engineering Corps as laborers.

THE REBEL ALLIANCE

The directive concerning these traitors is universal. Capture the high-ranking members for interrogation by the ISB. Exterminate the rest.

As the fortunes of war have shifted, this factor is beginning to work in the Alliance's favor. —Mothma

MILITARY RECRUITMENT

—NEXT-GENERATION THINKING—

The Imperial military is powerful, but its continued strength is only possible by recruiting and training the next generation of officers.

As an officer yourself, you know the sharp difference between those who lead and the rank and file. <u>Superior officers are a product of the academy system.</u>

The academy system predates the Imperial era. Under the misrule of the Old Republic, the academies atrophied. They were reduced to sorry shells of their former glory, turning out graduates to feed the meager forces of the Judicial Department and the Merchant Services.

The Empire restored the academy system and their proud traditions. Training facilities for the Navy, Army, and Stormtrooper Corps exist on dozens of worlds. Some are classified and known only to the members of Imperial Command, while others are renowned, their names celebrated across the galaxy for centuries.

NAVAL ACADEMIES

Officers in the Imperial Navy are trained at Sector Naval Academies for commissioning as lieutenants. Promising cadets are enrolled at one of the elite Naval Academies, where graduates may rise to the rank of TIE flight leader or Star Destroyer captain.

PREFSBELT IV NAVAL ACADEMY: This prestigious fleet institution is modeled after the ancient warrior traditions of Coruscant. Its hangars and landing strips are constantly abuzz.

CORUSCANI PILOT INSTITUTE: The CPI is located on the Imperial throneworld. Due to its prominence, it commonly trains the children of famous military families.

ARMY OFFICER ACADEMIES

Army academies act similarly to the Naval system. Smaller sector academies feed the candidate pool from several renowned institutions.

RAITHAL ACADEMY: The Academy at Raithal is one of the oldest institutions in the galaxy. Renewed under

Now that's just a lot of bunk. Did they forget that I came through the academy system? —Han

Lots of good pilots came through Prefsbelt—Hobbie and Biggs, to name two. —Wedge

the Empire, Raithal boasts live-fire training grounds for AT-AT walkers and other heavy assault vehicles.

CORULAG IMPERIAL MILITARY ACADEMY: The world of Corulag possesses this prize among the Core Worlds. Although primarily an Army academy, the facility does train pilots as well. Subsidiary flight camps are located in orbit and on the surface of Corulag's moon.

STORMTROOPER ACADEMIES

Facilities for the training of stormtrooper officers have sprung up all across the galaxy, now that stormtrooper ranks are no longer filled with veteran clone soldiers. Those who enroll find that stormtrooper academies are notoriously unforgiving.

CARIDAN MILITARY ACADEMY: This institution has existed for centuries, yet under the Empire it has shifted its expertise toward stormtrooper training. The Academy at Carida boasts facilities spanning the entire planet. Its stronger-than-average gravity toughens future graduates.

ROYAL GUARD ACADEMY OF YINCHORR: This unforgiving planet has a fittingly severe training facility. The Yinchorr citadel instructs members of Palpatine's personal Royal Guard, while smaller complexes train officers of the Imperial riot troopers and other stormtrooper divisions. It is doubtful you are cleared to know more than general information about this institution.

"WE MOVE FORWARD AS ONE PEOPLE—THE IMPERIAL CITIZENS OF THE FIRST GALACTIC EMPIRE. WE WILL PREVAIL. TEN THOUSAND YEARS OF PEACE BEGIN TODAY."

—FROM THE TEXT OF EMPEROR PALPATINE'S INAUGURAL SPEECH, DELIVERED 16:5:24

My time at Raithal wasn't pleasant, but I left there a true soldier. —MADINE

THE FAMOUS LONG HALL OF THE RAITHAL ACADEMY, FOLLOWING ITS IMPERIAL REDEDICATION CEREMONY.

PART II

THE IMPERIAL NAVY

By Admiral Conan Antonio Motti

Service, Fealty, Fidelity. That is our motto, and it guides all dealings with the Imperial Navy whether you count yourself in our ranks or not.

The goal of the Imperial Navy is absolute dominance of known space. The functions of the Navy include:

» Blockading ports—preventing supplies from reaching a planet to cripple its ability to fight

» Bombarding planets—annihilating infrastructure with pinpoint precision from orbit

» Guarding shipping lanes—protecting upstanding commerce from pirates and smugglers as well as scaring the criminals into honest work

» Transporting other branches of the Imperial military—carrying them safely to their destination and supplying them with space and aerial support after their disembarkation

The Imperial Army soldiers see themselves as planetside problem solvers, and the stormtroopers consider themselves elite commandos, but witness the reach of the Imperial Navy. All is ours, both the worlds we defend and the unfathomable void that lies between them. With a single hyperspace jump, we can strike anywhere. Our warships are unequaled.

Never has our motto held more meaning. The Emperor has raised an uncompromising new dawn. Service, fealty, fidelity—for the glory of the Empire!

The Empire has the numbers advantage, to say nothing of their superiority in firepower. If the Alliance cannot win the clash of navies, it matters little what ground we hold.
—Mothma

HISTORY OF THE IMPERIAL NAVY

Since the ancient seas of Coruscant lapped arcadian shores, navies have provided transportation, security, and firepower. The Imperial Navy is still young, but its roots in the Republic Navy of the Clone Wars should come as no surprise. The Republic Navy, in turn, emerged from the Republic Judicial Department's quiet commerce patrols.

But what our Emperor has accomplished since the formation of the New Order is miraculous. Under its policy of aggressive militarization, the Imperial Navy has grown the most. Our reach has never been longer, and our grip has never been tighter.

Imperialization transformed the Republic Navy into a true fighting force. Under the Empire, local naval flotillas were absorbed into a single hierarchy, and shipyards from Kuat to Jaemus roared to life. New warships launched daily. Sleek, angular Imperial Star Destroyers replaced the scarred battle boats of the Clone Wars, and the TIE fighters became the Navy's signature starfighter.

The increased fortification couldn't have been timelier. Resistance against the Empire is no longer a mere nuisance. The Rebel Alliance is persistent, striking from hidden strongholds. The Rebels have acquired formidable assets such as needling, energy-shielded starfighters and Mon Calamari cruisers that rival our Star Destroyers in size.

The Rebel threat must be met with naval power. Only the Imperial Navy can find them, fight them, and finish them. Only then will we triumphantly patrol the starlanes in the name of Imperial peace.

GREW TOO FAST, I MIGHT ADD. THE EMPIRE IS TOP-HEAVY WITH WAR MACHINES, AND CAN NO LONGER CREW THEM OR FIX THEM. —RIEEKAN

THE IMPERIAL CREWER

Like most military branches, the Imperial Navy is only as strong as the men who wear its uniform. Whether a highly trained tactical pilot, a communication specialist, a docking technician, or an officer aboard a Star Destroyer, the members of our proud service are bound by the Imperial Naval Code:

I WILL HONOR THE EMPIRE IN
MY THOUGHTS AND ACTIONS

I WILL OBEY MY SUPERIORS

I WILL NEVER SHIRK FROM MY DUTIES

I WILL MAINTAIN IMPECCABLE STANDARDS
OF CONDUCT AND APPEARANCE

I WILL USE IMPERIAL RESOURCES
RESPONSIBLY

I WILL COMPLETE EVERY MISSION WITHOUT
HESITATION, AMBIGUITY, OR MERCY

I WILL RECOGNIZE THAT THE EMPIRE IS
GREATER THAN MYSELF AND BE WILLING TO
DIE IN ITS SERVICE

I WILL CALL OUT THOSE WHO DO NOT
LIVE UP TO THE STANDARDS OF
THE NAVAL CODE

Indoctrination like this is what we have to fight if we want to win hearts and minds. —Leia

As somebody who actually graduated from the academy, I can say that nobody really believes this stuff. Not even the guy who wrote it. —Han

This code unites us in a common cause—from our commissioned officers who command and direct our mighty vessels of war, to the warrant officer specialists (typically drawn from the lower ranks) who provide services including weapons maintenance, hangar repairs, propulsion engineering, sensor scanning, and more. Our crewmen are the foundation of the Imperial Navy.

In addition to these crewmen, the following personnel hold highly visible posts aboard Imperial warships:

NAVAL TROOPERS

These troopers serve as a ship's security detail. They engage in direct combat during boarding operations, or in the unlikely event that an enemy breaches the defenses of an Imperial warship. Naval troopers often work alongside stormtroopers during fast-strike operations.

IMPERIAL GUNNERS

These members of the Flight Branch operate heavy weapons aboard warships and battle stations. All Imperial gunners are trained on heavy, medium, and light turbolasers, ion cannons, tractor beams, and missile launchers. Their duties include tracking targets during combat, firing at targets, reloading ammunition, and preventing weapon overloads. Beneath the jutting shell of an Imperial gunner's helmet are polarized filters to shield against blinding flashes. The helmet's eye slit also displays computerized tracking data for the wearer.

TIE PILOTS

Don't be fooled by the helmets—TIE pilots are naval graduates, not stormtroopers. They are the best of the best, having endured a gauntlet of strategic and high-speed flight challenges that filtered out the weak. TIE pilots are a closely knit group and tend to keep social interactions within their own kind. Consider this an acceptable trade-off for their outstanding flight performance. TIE pilots regularly face impossible odds inside their recklessly agile, unshielded starships, yet they still come out on top.

Space combat is stressful enough. Can't imagine having to fly an unshielded rattletrap too. —Wedge

IMPERIAL NAVY UNIFORMS

The following reference will allow you to visually identify the various members of the Imperial Navy according to their particular branch of service.

NAVAL OFFICER

The gray-green uniform of an Imperial naval officer includes a double-breasted tunic, trousers, and cap. Only elite Grand Admirals are permitted to wear white uniforms. NOTE: See separate discussion for rank insignia distinctions.

NAVAL TROOPER

The all-black jumpsuit uniform denotes a naval trooper and is donned for security duties and direct combat situations.

During a boarding action, you're more likely to fight naval troopers than stormtroopers. —MADINE

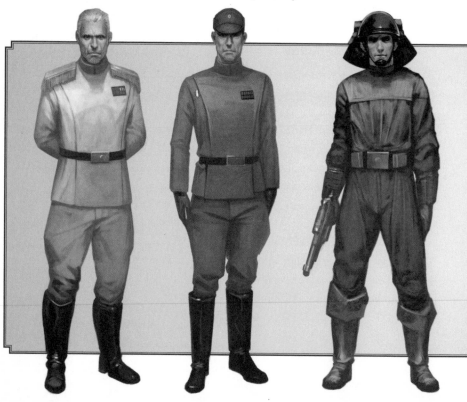

GRAND ADMIRAL   NAVAL OFFICER   NAVAL TROOPER

IMPERIAL GUNNER

The distinctive clamshell helmets and all-black duty uniforms make the gunners instantly identifiable.

TECHNICIANS

Specialists of this rank wear light gray or black jumpsuits with a shoulder patch and a forearm computer.

TIE PILOT

This all-black, environmentally sealed uniform features a life-support chestplate with attached breather tubes.

I've worn one of these. After a few hours in a cockpit, the stink of sweat and the hissing of the breathing tubes is enough to drive anybody crazy. —Han

IMPERIAL GUNNER   TIE PILOT   IMPERIAL TECHNICIAN

NAVAL OFFICER RANK INSIGNIA

An officer status within the Imperial Navy is be noted by a specific combination of rank squares and code cylinders displayed on the crewman's uniform.

Midshipman
DESCRIPTION: The lowest officer position in the Imperial Navy.
INSIGNIA: Two squares

Lieutenant
DESCRIPTION: Most officers aboard ship hold this position, which encompasses the ranks of Junior Lieutenant, Senior Lieutenant, and Junior Commander.
INSIGNIA: Four squares, one code cylinder

Captain
DESCRIPTION: The title held by a ship's commanding officer and includes the line rank of Senior Commander.
INSIGNIA: Six squares and one code cylinder

Admiral
DESCRIPTION: The position of Admiral is equivalent with the rank of Commodore. Informally, admirals may be addressed as commanders.
INSIGNIA: Eight squares, two code cylinders

Fleet Admiral
DESCRIPTION: The position held by the commander of a fleet, or the top military official within a planetary sector.
INSIGNIA: Ten squares, three code cylinders

High Admiral, Grand Admiral
DESCRIPTION: This elite rank is held only by those whom Emperor Palpatine has personally promoted. Grand Admirals wear white dress uniforms sometimes decorated with gold epaulets.
INSIGNIA: Twelve squares, four code cylinders

NAVAL RANK INSIGNIA
(post restructure)

MIDSHIPMAN

LIEUTENANT

CAPTAIN

ADMIRAL

FLEET ADMIRAL

HIGH
ADMIRAL

STRUCTURE AND ORGANIZATION

Naval Command is the organizing body that directs all operations for the Imperial Navy. It responds to the direct orders of Emperor Palpatine.

Under Naval Command, the Imperial Navy has four branches:

1. LINE BRANCH: Responsible for the Empire's warships, capital ships, and support ships, as well as their commanders and crew.

2. FLIGHT BRANCH: Responsible for the Empire's starfighters, their pilots, and support personnel.

3. FLEET SUPPORT BRANCH: Responsible for maintenance and engineering, including the Engineering Division and the Technical Services Division.

4. SUPPORT SERVICE BRANCH: Responsible for specialty systems including communications, navigation, weapons, and medical services.

FORMATIONS AND DEPLOYMENT

While all operations are directed by Naval Command, individual commanders have the Imperial armada at their disposal. They know better than to spend those resources recklessly. Not every situation calls for a hammer.

The Imperial naval force is composed of the following units:

LINE

STRUCTURE: Typically four larger ships, though this number can go as high as twenty depending on ship composition.

COMMANDER'S RANK: Captain (given the title Captain of the Line)

The line is the smallest organizational unit used for space combat.

» **ATTACK LINE:** Three heavy cruisers, or six to eight light cruisers. The attack line actively engages the enemy; if a Star Destroyer line is present to provide direct firepower, an attack line will harry the enemy's flanks.

» **HEAVY ATTACK LINE:** Four to eight medium or heavy cruisers, possibly including a Victory Star Destroyer.

» **STAR DESTROYER LINE**: A single Imperial Star Destroyer—by itself, this vessel is equivalent to a line in strength.

» **SKIRMISH LINE**: Four to twenty corvettes or similarly small, well-armed ships. A skirmish line engages starfighters and frigates as well as provides backup for TIE fighters.

» **PURSUIT LINE**: Four to ten light cruisers or frigates with enough speed capability to pursue fleeing ships.

» **TROOP LINE**: Two assault transports and two medium cruisers, used for ferrying Imperial Army troopers into active battlefields.

» **RECON LINE**: Two to four light cruisers fitted with surveillance and communications gear. Recon lines do not engage in direct combat but are critical in identifying the locations of Rebel hideouts.

SQUADRON

COMPOSITION: Multiple lines, typically totaling between fourteen to sixty ships.

COMMANDER'S RANK: Admiral

A squadron is the standard unit assigned to a single star system.

» **LIGHT SQUADRON**: One skirmish line and one reconnaissance line, assigned to low-threat systems.

A SUPERIORITY FLEET ENCIRCLES A TARGET WORLD, LEAVING ITS POPULATION NO MEANS OF ESCAPE.

INNOVATIONS IN IMPERIAL NAVAL TACTICS

By Captain Kendal Ozzel

I am not the first Ozzel to rise within the naval ranks. Perhaps you have read of Ruthbert Ozzel, the Savior of Mittoblade, or of Enos Ozzel who pushed the Cold Coil back into the Unknown Regions at the dawn of the Early Manderon Period. I share with my ancestors a quick mind and a deep intellect, which I have used to help codify Imperial naval tactics.

Innovation #1: Surprise. Emerge from hyperspace right on top of your enemy! Our navigators are capable of pinpoint calculations, so do not worry about overshooting your target. A surprised enemy will be unable to counter your offensive move. (See Fig 1.)

Innovation #2: Pursue. If the enemy flees, chase them! Star Destroyers are exceedingly speedy at sublight. Your engines can outrun any smuggling junker, so don't be afraid to light the fires. (See Fig 2.)

Innovation #3: Overwhelm. Use all your forces at once! Their combined firepower will more than make up for any loss of maneuverability. (See Fig 3.)

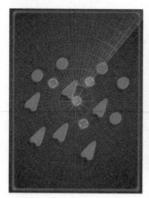

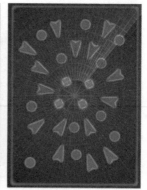

FIG 1   FIG 2   FIG 3

I can't make fun of this. It's just too easy. —Han

» HEAVY SQUADRON: Two heavy attack lines, assigned to systems with suspected enemy activity. In situations where pinpointing an enemy's position is required, the heavy squadron may be one attack line and one reconnaissance line. During aggressive operations against an enemy, it may be three heavy attack lines and one skirmish line.

» BATTLE SQUADRON: Two attack lines and one pursuit line, including at least one Imperial Star Destroyer. A battle squadron is typically used for offensive operations against a known enemy.

» BOMBARD SQUADRON: One skirmish line and one pursuit line, including at least one torpedo sphere (see Part V for more information on torpedo spheres). This type of squadron is used to penetrate planetary shields and quell active uprisings on rebellious worlds.

SYSTEMS FORCE

COMPOSITION: Multiple squadrons, typically totaling up to ninety ships

COMMANDER'S RANK: Systems Admiral (given the title of Commodore)

A systems force is responsible for maintaining order across several star systems.

» SUPERIORITY FORCE: Three battle squadrons and a light squadron assigned to maintain superiority in a given system.

» ESCORT FORCE: Two heavy squadrons and two light squadrons whose primary objective is to protect valuable Imperial assets.

» TRANSPORT FORCE: Two troop squadrons, one heavy squadron, and one light squadron employed to transport and deploy Army troops and stormtroopers.

» SYSTEM BOMBARD: Three bombard squadrons and one light squadron tasked with carrying out planetary bombardment missions.

» FORCE TECHNICAL SERVICES: Eight transports and two armed escort frigates, charged with transporting mechanical specialists quickly and safely wherever they are needed most.

» SUPPORT FORCE: Over a hundred container vessels tasked with resupplying Imperial depots across the galaxy.

FLEET

COMPOSITION: Multiple systems forces, typically totaling up to four hundred ships

COMMANDER'S RANK: Admiral (also given the title of Commodore)

A fleet typically operates within a single sector, but it does not represent all of a sector's naval resources.

» **SUPERIORITY FLEET:** Six Imperial Star Destroyers and up to four hundred support ships dispatched to low-threat sectors.

» **ASSAULT FLEET:** Two transport forces and two escort forces tasked to transport Imperial Army troopers to hostile sectors.

» **BOMBARD FLEET:** Two system bombards and two escort forces assigned to high-threat, low-value sectors. Bombard fleets annihilate opposition without concern for the local infrastructure.

» **SUPPORT FLEET:** Five hundred small vessels, most of them container ships. A support fleet equips Imperial military forces with weapons, ammunition, equipment, supplies, and consumables.

» **DEEPDOCK FLEET:** A total of 280 support vessels and one escort force, used to support two space-based shipyards. These "deepdock complexes" have over a hundred repair bays with hyperdrive engines for easy relocation.

SECTOR GROUP

COMPOSITION: Multiple fleets, typically at least 2,400 ships

COMMANDER'S RANK: High Admiral or Sector Moff

A sector group represents the totality of all naval forces within a sector and includes at least twenty-four Star Destroyers.

Even larger naval forces than the sector group can be assembled as regional groups or Oversector groups, but these are not part of the standard Order of Battle.

DISABLE THE DEEPDOCK FLEETS AND WE PREVENT IMPERIAL FLEETS FROM REPAIRING DAMAGE. I'VE DRAWN UP A PLAN TO HIT THE VORZYD SECTOR. —WEEKAN

WHAT YOU DON'T SEE: CLOAKING DEVICES

By Grand Admiral Martio Batch

Cloaking devices have never been common, but today they are practically non-existent. If you encounter one—and if it is working properly—it will block all methods of electromagnetic detection from the starship upon which it is installed, including visible light. No, it is not magic. It is, however, quite expensive. For decades, cloaking devices have been powered by stygian crystals mined from the Dreighton Nebula. Because that supply of crystals has nearly run dry, the use of cloaking devices has diminished.

Several Imperial vessels possess functional cloaks, though their identities are classified. A few cloaks still remain in private hands. As it requires a great amount of power to run an invisibility screen, a civilian cloak is likely to be found aboard a large freighter or a container ship. If you encounter one, dispose of its crew as necessary, but make every effort to capture the vessel intact.

Research continues into alternate power materials, while the Dreighton Nebula remains under martial quarantine.

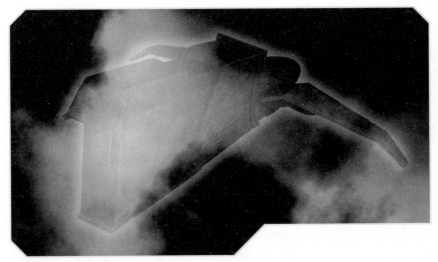

A cloaking device is an inscrutable piece of technology to those who haven't been trained in its maintenance. Only specialized Imperial technicians are certified to repair cloaking devices.

IMPERIAL NAVY SHIPS OF THE FLEET

The Empire's vessels are the greatest in the galaxy and are regularly deployed into action. Most Imperial warships were built within the last ten years.

Their modernity and technology is matched only by their staggering power and size. Most of the older civilian capital ships traveling the space-lanes, such as corvettes and frigates, measure between 100–600 meters. The heavy cruisers introduced during the Clone Wars, such as the Acclamator assault ship and the Victory Star Destroyer, measure 750–900 meters, and are still in limited use today.

However the ships of the modern Imperial Navy are far larger and far more capable. An Imperial Star Destroyer measures 1,600 meters from stem to stern, and some of the dreadnaughts planned for deployment in the coming years will dwarf even these.

STAR DESTROYERS

The Star Destroyer is the primary, capital warship of the Empire. Its triangular shape is a refinement of the Acclamator, Venator, and Victory Star Destroyer designs. In addition, its sharp silhouette has become a symbol of Imperial power.

IMPERIAL STAR DESTROYER (ISD)

A piercing weapon stabbing from the blackness, the 1,600-meter Imperial Star Destroyer is the pride of the Imperial Navy. Manufactured at Kuat Drive Yards for nearly two decades, these vessels patrol Imperial space in numbers exceeding the tens of thousands.

An Imperial Star Destroyer requires a crew of nearly 37,000 men. Each vessel has enough capacity to carry twenty AT-ATs and many smaller walkers, as well as the dropships needed to deliver them planetside. An ISD can also transport up to 9,700 ground troops.

The weapons of an Imperial Star Destroyer are infamous, capable of reducing a planetary surface to molten slag. Six heavy turbolaser turrets and two heavy ion cannon turrets make up the ship's main battery. Numerous smaller turbolasers spaced along the ship's hull create a screen of defense against starfighter attack. Ion cannons and tractor beam projectors offer further protection.

If the Empire fragments, there is a risk every commander with a Star Destroyer will become a warlord. —Mother

IMPERIAL STAR DESTROYER INFERNO

Imperial Star Destroyers also serve as starfighter carriers. A TIE wing—six squadrons, totaling seventy-two fighters—is an ISD's standard complement, including a mix of fighters, interceptors, and bombers. TIE fighters, shuttles, gunboats, and other vessels launch from the hangar on the ship's underside, which is large enough to swallow any captured freighters and corvettes.

A solar ionization reactor powers an ISD's three ion engines and four supplemental thrusters. These ships are remarkably fast at sublight speeds. Atop the bridge tower sit two sensor and communications globes, which also double as shield generators.

Imperial Star Destroyers are the Empire's primary battleship and are the building block for sector groups and battle squadrons.

VICTORY STAR DESTROYER (VSD)

Imperial Star Destroyers would not exist without this forerunner, which launched into service during the height of the Clone Wars. Measuring 900 meters, the Victory I and Victory II models are formidable warships that serve as support for the ISDs. However in the Rim, it is common to see VSDs operating alone against pirate marauders.

Standard Victory weaponry includes ten quad turbolaser batteries, forty double turbolaser batteries, eighty concussion missile tubes, and ten tractor beam projectors. A VSD crew numbers between 5,000–6,000. The ships are often used as transports as they can carry over 2,000 troopers.

The tactical advantage of a Victory Star Destroyer lies in its hyperdrive, which allows it to cross the galaxy in half the time of an Imperial Star

Destroyer. However, its sublight engines are noticeably slower, allowing most Rebel ships to quickly outpace a VSD.

Unlike their larger cousins, Victory Star Destroyers operate well inside planetary atmospheres. It is a glorious thing to witness a VSD making a strafing run in support of Imperial infantry.

INTERDICTOR CRUISER

Interdictors serve a vital role in the Imperial fleet by blocking the enemy from hyperspace. The most common Interdictor in service is the 600-meter Immobilizer 418, though Imperial Star Destroyers have also been refitted as Interdictor models.

By projecting a mass shadow from its gravity-well projectors, an Interdictor simulates a large planetary body on the extra-dimensional fabric of hyperspace. In practical terms, this prevents any ship from entering hyperspace within the Interdictor's gravity range. Additionally, if any ship's path intersects with the mass shadow, it will be forced out of hyperspace and into real space.

Interdictors are used primarily to patrol trade routes and enforce customs checkpoints. These random traffic inspections help discourage smuggling. Once an inspected vessel is given the all-clear, it is released from the grip of the Interdictor.

The Rebel Alliance's hyperspace-capable starfighters make the Interdictor's role more important than ever. An Interdictor can effectively cut off their escape route. No longer can a Rebel ambush flee to safety at the first sign of trouble.

SUPER STAR DESTROYER (SSD)

This warship is not yet in service, but it soon will be. The inaugural ships are taking shape at Kuat Drive Yards and the Fondor shipyards. Filling the role of a starship dreadnought, the 19,000-meter Super Star Destroyer will be the Empire's premier heavy warship and sector command vessel.

A Super Star Destroyer will require a crew of more than 280,000. Thirteen engines will propel the ship at sublight speed, providing acceleration far more rapid than its size would indicate. The Super Star Destroyer's weapons will include over 5,000 turbolaser and ion cannon batteries as well as 250 concussion missile launchers arranged at points along the ship's hull and within the ship's midline trenches.

If the Empire knew how to build smart—not just big—they would have made thousands more Interdictors. If they had, we might not have survived. —Leia

A dilemma. If the Alliance were to capture one of these behemoths, we wouldn't have enough personnel to crew it —Mothma

42

Super Star Destroyers will function as the Empire's primary TIE fighter carrier, troop transport, naval battleship, and planetary bombardment platform. The Emperor's ultimate vision is one SSD per sector, to serve as a command ship for Imperial forces.

SOVEREIGN- AND ECLIPSE-CLASS SUPER STAR DESTROYERS

Though still under development, these ship classes will revolutionize naval combat and ensure the Imperial Navy's dominance through the next century.

The *Eclipse*-class is planned at 17,500 meters in length. It will incorporate an axial superlaser to penetrate planetary shields and vaporize cities with a single blast. Planned subsidiary weapons systems include turbolasers, ion cannons, and tractor beam projectors, as well as the same gravity-well projectors used by Interdictor Star Destroyers.

The massive fore section of the *Eclipse*-class will have a hull so thick it can ram enemy vessels with impunity. It is estimated the vessel will require a crew of nearly 700,000.

Given its smaller size, the related *Sovereign*-class may come into service first. The *Sovereign* will measure 15,000 meters, which is the minimum space required to house the generators that power an axial superlaser. The ship is estimated to require a crew of 600,000.

I HAVEN'T HEARD ANYTHING ABOUT EITHER OF THESE. POSSIBLY A PROJECT THAT NEVER GOT OFF THE GROUND.
—RIEEKAN

SUPER STAR DESTROYER EXECUTOR

Naval Droids: Built to Serve

Imperial warships are complex, densely populated, mobile cities. Many corporations manufacture droid varieties for near-exclusive use by the Imperial Navy.

Self destructs if you tag it, so keep your head down. —Han

MODEL: MSE-6
MANUFACTURER: Rebaxan Columni

Nicknamed the mouse droid, the MSE is a nimble courier that delivers secure point-to-point communiqués. MSEs are also used for simple maintenance tasks including floor polishing and spot welding. If you see these droids zip by, give them a wide berth. It is best not to interfere with its high-priority delivery.

MODEL: RA-7
MANUFACTURER: Arakyd Industries

This protocol droid is frequently used as an officer's adjutant. RA-7 units keep timetables and maintain schedules, as well as act as translators when foreign emissaries are welcomed aboard ship.

MODEL: Viper Probot
MANUFACTURER: Arakyd Industries

Star Destroyers can carry hundreds of these probe droids, which are launched in rocket pods and operate autonomously once they reach their destination. The spider-like Viper has multiple low-hanging clawlike arms, a defensive laser cannon, and a multi-spectrum scanning package. Once its objective is achieved, it transmits the encoded findings along secure Imperial wavelengths.

MODEL: R-Series
MANUFACTURER: Industrial Automaton

Painted in naval black and gray, astromech droids operate in Imperial hangar bays to repair and maintain TIE fighters and shuttles, or in engine rooms to calculate hyperspace coordinates and provide updated navigational data.

IMPERIAL SUPPORT VESSELS

Star Destroyers are generally too large to make planetary landings. The Imperial Navy employs many types of shuttles and transports to move personnel and equipment from a Destroyer to a planet's surface, or to make transfers between ships of the fleet.

Imperial shuttle

The *Lambda*-class T-4a is the Navy's most common hyperspace shuttle and general-purpose light craft. It is frequently used as an officers' transport.

The shuttle's tri-wing design incorporates a large, fixed fin on the dorsal surface, with two additional wings that fold up against the central fin when the shuttle is docked. In flight, these wings extend downward into a three-point configuration.

A shuttle's standard weaponry consists of two forward-mounted, double-blaster cannons, one rear-mounted, double-blaster cannon, and two forward-mounted, double-laser cannons. An armored hull and a deflector shield generator protect the shuttle's occupants.

The *Lambda* can carry up to twenty passengers and has a standard crew of six: pilot, co-pilot, navigator, communications officer, gunner, and engineer.

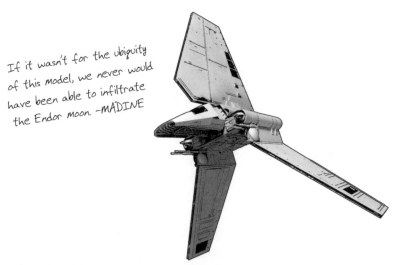

If it wasn't for the ubiquity of this model, we never would have been able to infiltrate the Endor moon. —MADINE

THE *Lambda*-CLASS IMPERIAL SHUTTLE IS HEAVILY SHIELDED, UNLIKE THE TIEs FREQUENTLY PRESSED INTO ESCORT SERVICE.

Sentinels are slow, but their weapons offer a full range of fire. It doesn't matter that an X-wing can overtake them, not when there isn't a safe approach vector. —Wedge

Don't neglect the Sentinel's offensive capabilities. It is well equipped for both delivery and pacification.

Sentinel landing craft

The Sentinel is the standard heavy transport used by the Imperial Navy. Its folding wing design and cockpit shape are similar to those of the *Lambda*-class Imperial shuttle.

With heavy armor plating and four deflector shield projectors, the Sentinel can transport troops into an active war zone, and then remain behind to provide aerial combat support if needed. A Sentinel can carry fifty-four troopers with speeder bikes and heavy equipment; and by reconfiguring the cargo compartment, a Sentinel can carry up to an additional twelve AT-ST scout walkers.

A Sentinel's weapons array consists of eight laser cannons, two concussion missile launchers, a retractable ion cannon, and two rotating repeating blasters. The craft's standard crew is one pilot, a co-pilot/sensor officer, and three gunners.

Walker dropship

The Y-85 Titan dropship deploys AT-AT walkers from Imperial naval warships down to planetary surfaces. Its heavy armor allows it to withstand sustained enemy fire during its descent, positioning maneuvers, and cargo unload. Two forward-facing twin laser cannons provide additional defenses.

A walker dropship can carry four AT-ATs and four AT-STs at a time. Within the craft, walkers are clamped into place by cranes so they can be deployed quickly from floor hatches.

Imperial freighter

This naval refitting of the Gozanti cruiser spaceframe allows for the transport of TIE fighters, AT-DP walkers, and stormtroopers between fleets and planetary garrisons. The freighter can carry up to four TIEs mounted beneath its wings, and act as a dropship for troopers and walkers in active battle zones.

TIE STARFIGHTERS

Under the Empire, starfighter development has flourished. The TIE series may be a checklist of familiar design elements—solar panel wings, eyeball cockpit, screaming ion engines—but it has served as a test bed for revolutionary experimentation.

Developed by Santhe/Sienar, the TIE series is named for the twin ion engines that propel it. These engines are fed by a solar ionization reactor, which draws power from the signature solar arrays.

Most TIEs do not have shields or hyperdrives. Because these features increase cost, adding them would reduce the Empire's ability to deploy TIEs in overwhelming numbers. TIE pilots are uniquely trained to avoid getting hit.

TIE fighter

The TIE fighter is the mainstay of the Imperial Flight Branch and the foundation for all the TIE variants.

Its engine is a marvel of precision design and requires little in the way of maintenance or tuning. The TIE fighter's lack of shields, life-support systems, or hyperdrive engines dramatically reduces its mass and results in a nimble, responsive craft.

The TIE fighter's weapons include a pair of laser cannons mounted on the chin of the cockpit. TIE fighters attack in large numbers to make up for any deficiencies in firepower or defensive strength. Imperial Command consider TIE fighters an inexpensive, expendable asset. The lack of a hyperdrive means TIE fighters are dependent on Star Destroyers or other carriers to ferry them into battle. TIE fighters can also be deployed groundside at Imperial garrisons, but their hexagonal wings can be a liability under windy conditions.

Eyeballs—that's what Alliance pilots call TIE fighters. Our comm chatter is a lot easier to understand when you know that. —Wedge

TIE BOMBER

One variant of the TIE bomber replaces the warhead bay with a cargo bay for passengers. Another variant features docking clamps and a hull cutter, and is used to transport stormtrooper boarding parties into action against hostile vessels.

TIE bomber

In addition to its signature bent-wings, TIE bombers have two elongated spaceframe pods—one for the pilot and one for the payload.

TIE bombers are utilized in surface assaults and offensive operations against capital ships. They are slower and less maneuverable than other TIE series models, but they can engage enemy starfighters from a distance by locking onto them with homing missiles. Like the TIE fighter, bombers also possess a pair of forward-facing laser cannons.

The ordnance pod of a TIE bomber can carry a variety of warheads. Common payloads include sixteen concussion missiles, twelve proton torpedoes, eight proton rockets, six space mines, four proton bombs, or sixty-four thermal detonators. The bomber's sensor package actively resists hostile electronic jamming.

Dupes handle like a walker hip-deep in mud, but those homing missiles are a real pain. It's tough to break a lock, especially when you've got an interceptor on your tail. —Wedge

TIE interceptor

One of the fastest starfighters in existence, the TIE interceptor is identifiable by its dagger-shaped solar arrays. Its angled panels jut forward, but cutaways on either side provide the pilot with peripheral visibility. Most TIE interceptors have four laser cannons, one on each wingtip. Others use the two chin-mounted lasers found on the standard TIE fighter.

Designed to outrun and outmaneuver enemy starfighters, the TIE interceptor features an advanced ion-stream projector that enables in complex combat maneuvers. The craft has earned praise from the Flight Branch. The

And these, we call squints. Somebody has to preserve the squadron lingo. —Wedge

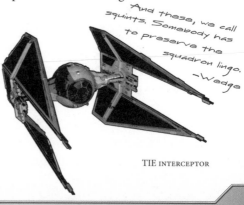

TIE INTERCEPTOR

distinguished 128th TIE Interceptor Squadron under Lieutenant Kasan Moor is one example of what the Empire can achieve when the best pilots are given the best machines.

TIE Advanced

The TIE Advanced is still in prototype, but an early model is now in the hands of Lord Darth Vader as his personal starfighter. The craft was built by chief engineer Raith Sienar according to Vader's specifications, and the Dark Lord's positive reaction to the design has raised hopes that it will be produced in greater numbers.

The craft has an elongated spaceframe and a reinforced hull, with solar arrays angled toward the body of the ship to create a compact profile. It also features two heavy laser cannons and a missile launcher.

Most notably, the TIE Advanced incorporates a shield generator and a hyperdrive. This dramatically increases its cost, but hopefully these improvements will boost performance at a commensurate level.

Early TIE Advanced prototypes exist in limited quantities. Gifted to the Emperor's Inquisitors and other favored acolytes, these special ships can be identified by their more compact wing panel configuration and thus smaller silhouettes.

TIE FIGHTER. NOTE THE SMALLER SOLAR ARRAYS.

SPECIAL SECTION:
EXPERIMENTAL TIE MODELS

By Captain Soontir Fel

I am a pilot, not an engineer. When it comes to the TIE series, I may not be qualified to speak to their costs or compromises. But I have flown them, and I know their tolerances. In my brief time at the Imperial Classified Flight Yards, I put all of these models through their paces. These TIEs are either in limited release now, or they will be soon.

TIE Aggressor

The Aggressor is a strike fighter with heavy ordnance, which classifies it as a hybrid fighter/bomber. Its forward-facing armament consists of two low-slung laser cannons and one missile launcher.

TIE AGGRESSOR

The Aggressor has a crew of two: a pilot and a gunner. The latter operates the laser turret mounted at the back of the craft's spaceframe. With this configuration, the Aggressor can pick off pursuers who try to take advantage of the TIE's traditional blind spot.

Though the craft lacks a hyperdrive, its supply of fuel and consumables allows it to operate for multi-day missions within a single star system. In the Outer Rim, the Aggressor is already being used to harass Rebel shipping.

THESE DON'T HANDLE MUCH BETTER THAN Y-WINGS, AND THEY DON'T HAVE A SHIELD GENERATOR EITHER. WATCH YOUR APPROACH ANGLES AND YOU SHOULD BE ABLE TO GET THE DROP ON THEM. —LUKE

TIE Hunter

The TIE Hunter, commissioned by the Empire's storm commandos, is intended to counter every advantage the Rebel Alliance's X-wing fighters may possess. The solar panels on the Hunter open and close like the S-foils of an X-wing, and extend in attack mode to provide larger coverage for the Hunter's laser cannons.

TIE HUNTER

The Hunter has a shield generator and hyperdrive, and can operate independently of a carrier. It is extremely fast at sublight. Its weapons complement consists of two laser cannons, two ion cannons, and one proton torpedo launcher.

TIE Defender

Still in development, the TIE Defender promises to be the most revolutionary expression of the TIE series—assuming Sienar's engineers can figure out how to put the required firepower into such a small frame.

TIE DEFENDER

The TIE Defender is a shielded, hyperspace-capable starfighter, bearing a distinctive silhouette with its three angled solar panels.

Two laser cannons are mounted on the overhead wing, and two more are mounted on each of the remaining wings. The Defender also comes with two warhead launchers for firing concussion missiles or proton torpedoes, and a tractor beam projector that can slow enemy craft enough to ensure a targeting lock.

The craft has an upgraded twin ion engine. Maneuvering jets, mounted on the tips of all three wings, give the Defender an uncanny degree of maneuverability.

The TIE Defender will be difficult for most operators to handle, given its power and its multiple weapons systems. To entrust its controls to anyone other than an elite pilot would be a mistake.

TIE Phantom

The TIE Phantom is currently under development at a classified location. This prototype starfighter is a modified version of the V38 assault fighter. It is equipped with a hyperdrive and a shield generator, but it is truly remarkable for its cloaking device.

TIE PHANTOM

Based on classified technology, the cloak offers total invisibility to electronic sensors and the naked eye. The cloak works in tandem with the weapons system, dropping for a split second every time the weapons fire.

The Phantom's weapons consist of two laser cannons on the fuselage and three laser cannons on the tips of the wings. The solar panel wings jut directly out from the fuselage like the fins of a krakana. Its elongated cockpit features life-supporting atmospheric circulation.

The TIE Phantom is equipped with enough supplies for long-range operations. Yet its weapons complement classifies it as an attack starfighter. It goes without saying that the Phantom could be the perfect stealth and reconnaissance craft.

DEEP SPACE HAZARDS: VACUUM-BASED WILDLIFE

By Crew Chief Oxenbrigg

I oversee a naval hull-integrity maintenance crew. If we do our jobs properly, you won't even notice us. But there are a few things you can do to keep your vessel in peak fighting shape and to make our jobs a little easier.

Animals are rare in the vacuum interstellar space, but they're out there. I mean, you'd never think a sand dune or a frozen glacier has anything alive underneath it until something jumps out and bites you. It's exactly the same out in the void.

Mynocks: Batlike scavengers. Wingspans are usually one to two meters. They feed on energy and multiply by splitting off little buds of themselves. Their normal diet is whatever faint traces of stellar and cosmic radiation waft their way, so a starship's reactor is like a feast to them.

Mynock

If you stay too long in orbit or dock at any space station unrated by Imperial Ships & Services, you'll probably find mynocks. If my crew and I don't get to them first, they can burrow into your hull and chew through your power lines.

Space slugs: Big worms with teeth. Usually about ten meters long, but veteran spacers claim they've seen ones a hundred times that size. Space slugs live in caverns on airless moons and asteroids. Usually, like mynocks, they passively feed on radiation. But space slugs will happily chomp rock and metal. It's why they've got those big chompers!

Space slug

Avoid asteroid fields, and be prepared to fire at any space slug that gets close. Once they attach to your ship, they're almost impossible to dislodge. Repairing bite marks is not any fun either.

MISSION REPORT: THE BATTLE OF TURKANA

Countering Fast-Attack Starfighters is Critical for Victory

By Captain Firmus Piett, Star Destroyer *Accuser*

Turkana is a sparsely populated world in the Pakuuni sector near the Tion Cluster. Imperial Intelligence reported a concentration of Rebel warships orbiting the planet. Initial estimates ranged between four to six capital ships and three to eight smaller vessels. The sector governor deployed ten Imperial Star Destroyers to Turkana with orders to trap and eliminate the threat.

The Star Destroyer *Tyrant*, under the command of Captain Lennox, served as lead vessel. The Star Destroyer *Accuser*, under my command, provided primary support for the *Tyrant*.

After verifying the enemy's position with a starfighter flyby, our fleet dropped from hyperspace to surprise the rebels and block their hyperspace escape vector (Formation Besh, Attack Pattern Tartarus). The actual enemy composition at the time of our arrival consisted of seven Mon Calamari star cruisers, two Nebulon-B frigates, two CR-90 corvettes, four GR-75 medium transports, and one Golan Ribbon tanker presumably supplying fuel to the Rebel task force.

All Star Destroyers engaged the Rebel cruisers with long-range turbolasers. Captain Lennox ordered the *Tyrant*, *Accuser*, and *Flanchard* to launch their TIE starfighter wings. The TIE bombers targeted the engines of the enemy

cruisers. The TIE fighters and TIE interceptors provided cover to draw enemy starfighters away from the bombers.

Less than a minute into the battle, the Rebels launched their own starfighters. The enemy fighters consisted of three squadrons of BTL Y-wings and two squadrons of Incom's new T-65 X-wings.

I advised Captain Lennox of the advanced capabilities of the X-wings, but he remained firm that superior numbers would carry the day and did not modify his tactics. The X-wings closed with the TIEs and interceptors, negating their maneuverability with comparable speeds and turns. The X-wings also absorbed direct hits with their onboard energy shields. With our TIEs thus occupied, the Rebel Y-wings continued through the starfighter scrum and began to pick off our bombers one by one.

Believing that Captain Lennox's actions had already cost the Empire a victory, I positioned the *Accuser* to fire its turbolasers along the bombers' attack path. This vaporized many of the harassing Y-wings and allowed one bomber squadron to deliver its payload, disabling the sublight engines of one MC80 cruiser.

By this point, the X-wings had finished off our starfighters and joined with the Y-wings to target our remaining bombers. I ordered all Star Destroyers to close to full weapons range (Formation Aleph, Attack Pattern Abbadon). But without a starfighter screen, we could not prevent the Rebel starfighters from unloading their proton torpedoes against the bridge shields of the *Formidable* and the *Ajax*, severely damaging both vessels.

Lennox issued the order to retreat. The fleet jumped to hyperspace and regrouped at Pakuuni. Several Rebel capital ships suffered damage, but none were destroyed.

POST-MISSION RECOMMENDATIONS:

· Deploy fast-moving interceptors, in greater numbers, when facing Rebel X-wings

· Slow down enemy starfighters with tractor beams to assist our gunners in locking on small targets

· Remove Captain Lennox from command of Pakuuni sector naval operations. Note: I have prepared an appropriate campaign plan [refer to NFOp-TbM-11891: Operation Strike Fear] and am prepared to lead the Empire's counterattack.

Red Squadron was piloting twelve of those X-wings, stationed aboard Ackbar's ship Independence. I notched three kills before I had to eject.

—Wedge

PART III

THE IMPERIAL ARMY

By High General Cassio Tagge

The goal of the Imperial Army is surface superiority.

The reason for this goal is plain—we are living beings. We cannot survive in a cold vacuum, for we are not mynocks. Ask yourself, why do the empty spaces between the stars hold strategic value? It is only because the hyperlanes *lead* somewhere—to worlds fit for habitation, or exploitation of their resources. The Imperial Army captures and occupies these worlds in the name of the Emperor and defends them from aggression.

To the Imperial Navy who brings us to our battlefield—we are grateful for the ride, and we offer you our thanks. But only when the Imperial Army has disembarked does the war truly begin.

We are not the Stormtrooper Corps. You see stormtroopers blitzing enemy fortifications or establishing beachheads, but often at a heavy loss to their own lines. They have their role, and it is . . . consistent. The Imperial Army, and only the Imperial Army, is equipped to seize and defend a planet. Our specialized formations and heavy equipment may take longer to deploy, but we are capable of decisive planetary operations and sustained surface superiority.

The Imperial Army encompasses infantry, armored cavalry, special forces, artillery operators, engineers, scouts, and drivers. We are heirs to the noble profession of arms who serve His Imperial Majesty Emperor Palpatine and the precepts of his Galactic Empire.

NUMBERS. SHEER NUMBERS AND SUPERIOR EQUIPMENT. THE ALLIANCE CAN NEVER HOPE TO BEAT THE IMPERIAL ARMY IN OPEN COMBAT.
—RIEEKAN

HISTORY OF THE IMPERIAL ARMY

The Imperial Army has existed in its current form for less than two decades. Yet we soldiers share a bond with all fallen warriors. Since the first Taung chieftain raised his spear to signal a charge, soldiers have nobly shed blood for the glory of a greater cause.

The origins of the Imperial Army lie with the Grand Army of the Republic, assembled in a time of great need to protect a unified, just, and orderly galactic governance from the Separatist terror of the Confederacy of Independent Systems. Throughout the years of the Clone Wars, the Grand Army of the Republic enlisted volunteers, conscripts, and career military officers from the ranks of the Republic Judicial Forces to supplement the vat-grown clone troopers. After the war, the surviving clone troopers formed the backbone of the Stormtrooper Corps, leaving the Imperial Army clone-free and primed to dedicate itself to the mission of surface superiority.

Thanks to the acceleration of military research during wartime, the Imperial Army benefitted from inventive and destructive machines. The AT-TE provided the template for a wealth of new armored walker designs. So too did we gain new understanding into the science of warfare. The human commanders who led the clone troopers transitioned to elite officers within the Imperial Army, where their tactical experience vanquishing Separatist droids could be repurposed to bring lingering Separatist sympathizers in line.

The Imperial Army single-handedly silenced the threat of dissent in those early battles. We would gladly have shifted our focus to peacekeeping, but regrettably treason and cowardice took an ugly new shape—the Rebel Alliance.

Without regard for the safety of all true Imperial citizens, these vicious Rebels sowed their poison on thousands of worlds. Had it not been for the faithful soldiers who stepped up to preserve the New Order that Emperor Palpatine built, the virus would have spread, plunging the galaxy into utter chaos.

The Rebels, and those who claim kinship with them, fear order. They distrust prosperity. They hate progress.

They claim to be noble, but they deny responsibility for their actions. —Leia

It's just an empty boast. Besides, this guy is space dust now. —Han

Of all the blind, barbaric, half-witted statements, these are some of the vilest. Words have power. Propaganda like this makes our fight more difficult. It's slander and should not be dismissed lightly. —Leia

Look at who they welcome as soldiers and officers, and you will see faces that are furred, scaled, and goggle-eyed. From this, you will see that they hate Humans as well.

The Imperial Army is more vital than ever. Our current state of emergency will not end until the Rebel Alliance has met complete and utter annihilation.

VIGILANCE IS VICTORY.

THE IMPERIAL SOLDIER

A soldier of the Imperial Army is no ragged recruit from planetary militia. Our soldiers are the Empire's foremost defenders.

Every soldier of the Imperial Army must follow these four principles:

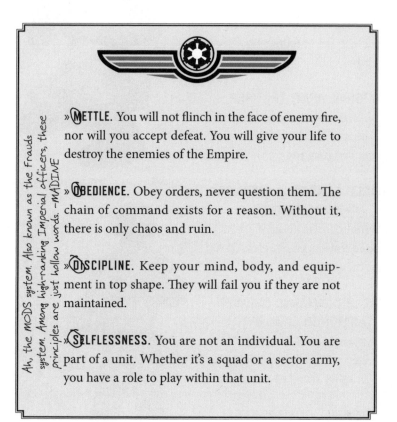

» **METTLE.** You will not flinch in the face of enemy fire, nor will you accept defeat. You will give your life to destroy the enemies of the Empire.

» **OBEDIENCE.** Obey orders, never question them. The chain of command exists for a reason. Without it, there is only chaos and ruin.

» **DISCIPLINE.** Keep your mind, body, and equipment in top shape. They will fail you if they are not maintained.

» **SELFLESSNESS.** You are not an individual. You are part of a unit. Whether it's a squad or a sector army, you have a role to play within that unit.

Ah, the MODS system. Also known as the frauds system. Among high-ranking Imperial officers, these principles are just hollow words. —MADINE

Remember, the Imperial Army fights to impose the Emperor's rule on planets from the Core to the Rim. We fight in diverse environments. We fight to break the enemy's will, and by their example we warn others of the futility of challenging the Empire.

We fight, and we win.

IMPERIAL ARMY UNIFORMS

Uniforms display our polished professionalism to the Emperor's subjects. Shown here are the correct uniforms for various divisions within the Imperial Army. As a commander, you should recognize these and call out soldiers who fail to follow regulation dress code.

IMPERIAL ARMY TROOPER
The uniform of an infantry trooper, heavy weapons trooper, and other common designations.

VEHICLE COMMAND CREWER (HEAVY ARMOR)
The armored battle dress of a vehicle command crewer operating an AT-AT or other heavy armor.

VEHICLE COMMAND CREWER (ARMORED CAVALRY)
The lightweight battle dress of a vehicle command crewer operating an AT-ST or other armored cavalry.

IMPERIAL COMMANDO
Commandos are exceptional Army officers who have been trained to execute assaults on high-value targets. Imperial commandos are an elite unit within the Army's Special Missions forces, and their uniforms reflect their status.

Vehicle command crewer (Heavy armor)

Doesn't offer much in the way of protection. Must be why they stay sealed up in their walking cans. ~Han

Vehicle command crewer (Armored cavalry)

MISSION STRUCTURE

The Imperial Army serves the Emperor. <u>We do not answer to civilians and are unconcerned with their complaints.</u> Orders come from the Emperor and are transmitted from Army Command down through a clear hierarchy.

How those orders convert into specific action is dependent on a commander's ability to follow protocol. What units will a commander deploy into battle? How are those units used within battle? The answers are determined by set objectives and available resources. The Imperial Army is charged with maintaining and enforcing the Empire's land-based superiority. Often the plans to enforce that power, either by seizing a single hill or subjugating an entire planet, rest upon the smart decisions of a unit commander.

Objectives for surface missions undertaken by the Imperial Army include the following:

» Obliterate an enemy possession utterly.

» Engage enemy infantry and mechanized units.

» Provide for the strategic insertion of commandos or expeditionary forces.

» Secure control of a key planetary resource or supply line.

» Hold an objective and destroy enemy attackers attempting to reclaim it.

As a commander, you are responsible for setting the terms of the battle. Once the parameters of engagement have been outlined, a commander must move swiftly and decisively. Initial response should overwhelm the enemy with firepower, leaving them shell-shocked and helpless. Once they are in disorder, strike to disrupt the enemy's plans and expose their flaws. Capture, hold, and capitalize on your objective! Never relent. Let your victory be a warning to anyone who doubts Imperial might.

While a resistant population is defined by its location and planet, the Rebel Alliance is a borderless enemy. They are cowards who strike from the void and rapidly melt back into nothingness.

[Handwritten left margin: That's no way to make local allies. Most Imperial Special Missions units don't think this way —MADINE]

[Handwritten right margin: This isn't a flaw, it's a feature. —Wedge]

When Rebels are discovered, the Imperial Army's first priority is to immediately and decisively eradicate their existence. Just as one might sterilize a wound by applying heat, a suspected Rebel cell operating in a populated city should be drawn out and then eliminated with extreme prejudice. The Imperial Army need not seek the cooperation of local planetary governments, but should requisition their obedience as necessary.

In addition to monitoring Rebel presence, an Imperial Army Commander is cognizant of the criminal underworld. Hutts, smugglers, bounty hunters, and others who live in civilization's fringes may not technically be part of the Rebels, but they are enemies of the Empire just the same.

FORMATIONS AND DEPLOYMENT

A commander must respond to threats with appropriate force. As the Imperial Army is structured to tackle any challenge, assessing what a situation requires—escalation, additional units, special units, etc.—is central to a commander's duties. Knowing the major unit groupings of the Imperial Army is vital.

SQUAD
STRUCTURE: Nine troopers
COMMANDER'S RANK: Sergeant
CAPABLE OF: Capturing a building

A squad is the smallest unit of the Imperial Army and core to its function. It consists of eight troopers plus a sergeant who is acting commander. Each squad can be subdivided into two fire teams under the sergeant's command. A squad's specialty training and equipment defines their military function. Currently, the Imperial Army contains the following types of squads:

» **LINE SQUAD:** The basic Imperial infantry unit.

» **HEAVY WEAPONS SQUAD:** The troopers of this unit are equipped with repeating blasters to provide front-line firepower.

» **SHARPSHOOTER SQUAD:** Equipped with sniper rifles, the members of this unit are drawn from the ranks of Special Missions forces.

THE EMPIRE CAN AFFORD TO FIELD SPECIALIZED TROOPERS IN GREAT NUMBERS. FORTUNATELY THEY ARE NOT AS WELL TRAINED AS WE ARE.
—RIEEKAN

I beg to differ. —MADINE

» **ENGINEERING SQUAD:** These troopers are demolitions and repair experts with extensive tech training and are also drawn from the ranks of Special Missions troopers.

» **REPULSORLIFT SQUAD:** Serving as drivers, gunners, and mechanics, this squad operates two light repulsorlift transports.

» **HEAVY WEAPONS REPULSORLIFT SQUAD:** The members of this squad handle two repulsorlift transports packed with extra firepower in the form of repeating blaster cannons or grenade launchers.

» **SCOUT SQUAD, OR LANCE:** The basic reconnaissance squad, or lance, of the Imperial Army consists of five troopers equipped with repulsorlift speeder bikes, or AT-RTs. Two scout lances combine to form a scout squadron.

PLATOON

STRUCTURE: Four squads
COMMANDER'S RANK: Lieutenant
CAPABLE OF: Capturing a district

Specialization at the platoon level offers a commander more options in aggressive action for a platoon's deployment may involve heavy armor (AT-ATs) and artillery pieces. Tactical platoons include:

» **LINE PLATOON:** The basic infantry formation composed of four infantry squads.

A PLATOON IS A NIMBLE AND EASILY CONFIGURABLE COMBAT UNIT. AVOID CALLING IN MORE FORCES THAN NECESSARY, UNLESS YOU WISH TO WASTE THE EMPEROR'S RESOURCES.

» **ASSAULT PLATOON:** This blended configuration combines two line squads with two heavy weapons squads. It can be augmented with armored vehicles.

» **ARTILLERY PLATOON:** An artillery platoon consists of four dedicated artillery pieces or eight artillery-equipped light vehicles, along with their crews. Long-range artillery is used to attack distant targets. The function of artillery can be line-of-sight direct fire (such as the V-188 Penetrator blaster or the Speizoc C-136 "Grandfather Gun" ion cannon), parabolic indirect fire (such as the MobileMortar-3), or anti-aircraft fire (such as the G-003 Tri-Tracker).

» **REPULSORLIFT PLATOON:** Composed of four repulsorlift squads, repulsorlift platoons are typically used for harassment skirmishes in an attempt to disrupt enemy front-line formations.

» **HEAVY WEAPONS REPULSORLIFT PLATOON:** Four heavy weapons repulsorlift squads combined create an ideal platoon to break through infantry lines.

» **ARMOR PLATOON:** An armor platoon consists of four heavy walkers such as AT-ATs or eight repulsorlift tanks. Each platoon is accompanied by two heavy transport vehicles for repair and resupply.

» **SPECIAL MISSIONS PLATOON:** This platoon has a variable configuration based on mission needs. A typical complement might number two sharpshooter squads, one engineering squad, and one heavy weapons squad.

» **SCOUT PLATOON:** Formed from the combination of two scout lances and two infantry line squads, a scout platoon specializes in reconnaissance missions, though during instances of comm-signal jamming, they are used to deliver messages.

COMPANY

STRUCTURE: Four platoons
COMMANDER'S RANK: Captain
CAPABLE OF: Capturing a city

A company is large enough to require the services of support personnel, including those assigned to the logistics, medical, and technical fields. Army companies also employ large numbers of military-issue droids to resupply troops in the field and to perform administrative functions at command posts.

» **LINE COMPANY:** The standard infantry company is frequently

The Alliance has acquired Imperial artillery pieces through combat, but we lack the crews to operate them. —Mothma augmented with one or more heavy weapons platoons.

» ASSAULT COMPANY/HEAVY WEAPONS COMPANY:
Two assault platoons and two line platoons combine to form this multipurpose surface unit.

» SCOUT COMPANY:
A cohesive group that consists of four scout platoons and their speeder bikes.

» REPULSORLIFT COMPANY:
This dedicated mechanized infantry unit is formed from two line platoons and two repulsorlift platoons. The repulsorlift vehicles carry infantry troopers into combat and provide fire support after troopers have dismounted.

» DROP COMPANY:
Capable of operating independently behind enemy lines, drop companies act as pathfinders, scouting out landing zones and resupply points that will be used later during full-scale invasions. Six-week missions often turn into six months for these inventive survivalists.

» ARTILLERY COMPANY/ARTILLERY BATTERY:
An artillery battery consists of sixteen heavy artillery pieces or thirty-two light artillery pieces.

» ARMOR COMPANY:
With a combination of heavy walkers and armored repulsortanks, these companies form a juggernaut of power. They can be arranged into two main punishing formations:

• ATTACK ARMOR COMPANY:
Three armor platoons and one heavy weapons platoon. Emphasis: Battlefield Versatility

• BREAKTHROUGH ARMOR COMPANY:
Four armor platoons. Emphasis: Concentrated Destruction

» SPECIAL MISSIONS COMPANY:
Designed to operate as an expeditionary force, this grouping merges three special missions platoons and one scout platoon. Known for tackling impossible tasks, the special missions company uses scout lances to identify the objective and Special Missions troopers to demolish the target.

BATTALION

STRUCTURE: Four companies
COMMANDER'S RANK: Major
CAPABLE OF: Capturing a major urban center

In our current war with the Rebel seditionists, a battalion is frequently assigned the role of planetary

i was shot down over Tieos. These are definitely not the guys you want to find you. —Wedge

suppression. In addition to standard and specialized companies, security personnel are also included in a battalion to maintain order within the ranks.

» **LINE BATTALION:** A standard battalion configuration is comprised of three line companies and one heavy weapons company.

» **ASSAULT BATTALION:** This integration of two heavy weapons companies, one repulsorlift company, and one line company is designed to storm enemy fortifications and breach defensive walls.

» **REPULSORLIFT BATTALION:** Three repulsorlift companies and a scout company provide easy mobility.

» **ARTILLERY BATTALION:** By joining one heavy weapons company to three artillery batteries, the heavy weapons troopers can deploy around the artillery pieces to protect them during firing.

» **ARMOR BATTALION:** One breakthrough armor company, two attack armor companies, and one repulsorlift company provide a versatile and mobile arrangement that has a reputation for surviving overwhelming odds.

» **SPECIAL MISSIONS BATTALION:** Four special missions companies comprise a special missions battalion. It is the largest configuration of special missions forces within the Imperial Army.

An Imperial Assault Regiment guarantees planetary neutralization.

REGIMENT

STRUCTURE: Four battalions
COMMANDER'S RANK: Lieutenant Colonel
CAPABLE OF: Capturing a territorial region

The regiment is a formidable army formation requiring extensive support and resupply. A regimental headquarters is equipped with its own manufacturing workshop to produce spare parts for walkers and additional components.

» **LINE REGIMENT:** Two line battalions, one assault battalion, and one repulsorlift battalion form a standard configuration considered appropriate for long-term occupation of a planetary region.

» **ASSAULT REGIMENT:** Two assault battalions, one line battalion, and one armor battalion constitute an assault regiment. There is very little, from Core to Rim, that can stand in their way.

» **REPULSORLIFT REGIMENT:** Fast-acting and responsive, a repulsorlift regiment consists of three repulsorlift battalions and one armor battalion.

» **ARTILLERY REGIMENT:** A typical artillery regiment is comprised of three artillery battalions and one assault battalion, augmented by a scout company. As the Rebel Alliance abandons their fortified holdings and scuttles into the shadows, the Imperial Army has been forced to reduce its reliance on artillery.

ARMOR REGIMENT: Few regions can withstand this hard-hitting combination of armor battalions and repulsorlift battalions. The 112th Repulsorlift Armor Regiment, better known as the "Hell's Hammers," is a famous example of a vanguard armor regiment.

BATTLEGROUP

STRUCTURE: Four regiments
COMMANDER'S RANK: Colonel
CAPABLE OF: Capturing a continent

An Imperial battlegroup is unstoppable. On a tactical holomap, commanders can watch as the visual indicator for a battlegroup gradually spreads across the terrain like spilled blood, changing the blue that indicates contested territory into victorious Imperial red. Coordinating battlegroups is critical if a commander wishes to put down multiple trouble spots on a contested planet.

» LINE BATTLEGROUP: A standard battlegroup configuration consisting of three line regiments and one assault regiment.

» ASSAULT/REINFORCED BATTLEGROUP: Composed of two line regiments, one assault regiment, and one armor regiment, this battlegroup offers a mix of specializations for diverse planetary environments. The 1st Tapani Assault Battlegroup has filled this role with distinction, notching Imperial victories during the Rout of Spuma and the Humiliation of Barkhesh.

» ARMOR BATTLEGROUP: Composed of four armor regiments, this battlegroup is unmatched when it comes to blasting apart concentrated knots of resistance.

» MOBILE BATTLEGROUP: Three repulsorlift regiments and one line regiment provide a swift way to mobilize mechanized infantry.

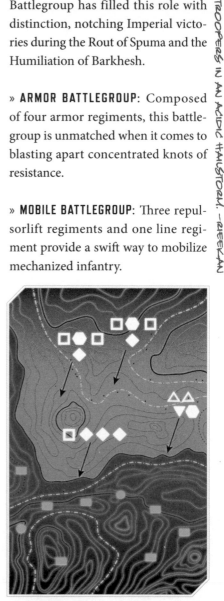

A BATTLEGROUP IS A TREMENDOUS OUTLAY OF IMPERIAL RESOURCES. DEPLOY IT WISELY.

PATHS TO VICTORY: USING NATIVE FORCES TO YOUR ADVANTAGE

By General Rom Mohc

Consider, if you will, the Ailon Nova Guard. They are fierce fighters
who are also highly disciplined, and in my experience the latter is
a rare quality among non-Humans. Because our Emperor has seen fit to
humor the Ailons by participating in their parades and military cel-
ebrations, they have developed a worshipful reverence for the Emperor
and the army he commands. Thus, the billion warriors who make up the
Ailon Nova Guard will rush blindly into no-win combat situations if
ordered to do so by an
Imperial commander.

I have used the Nova Guard
as disposable assets on
many occasions. Tactical
analysis of their deaths
provides real-time intel-
ligence on the firepower
and location of hostile gun
emplacements. Such data
allows Imperial forces to
capture an objective with
minimal loss of life.

If the Ailon Nova Guard
should somehow succeed in
their objective (which did
in fact occur during the
Sundering of Slession),
these assets can be pre-
served for their next
mission. *Appallingly callous. Let us extend the
hand of the Alliance to the people of Ailon.
—Leia*

*It may be of little comfort, but General Mohc
has been dealt with. —Mothma*

Ailon Nova Guard

CORPS

STRUCTURE: Four battlegroups
COMMANDER'S RANK: Major General
CAPABLE OF: Capturing a planet

At the corps level, commanders can expect to see increased input from Imperial Intelligence agents and the Emperor's political advisors. The headquarters of a corps is a busy complex that incorporates an automated manufacturing facility. The configuration or type of corps deployed depends on the planetary environment, population, and level of hostility.

» **LINE CORPS:** A standard configuration of three line battlegroups and one assault battlegroup.

» **ATRISIAN CORPS:** Named in honor of the ancient Atrisian warriors of the Kitel Phard Dynasty, this configuration is composed of two assault battlegroups, one line battlegroup, and one armor battlegroup.

» **ARMOR CORPS:** Heavy on offensive power, an armor corps is three armor battlegroups and one mobile battlegroup.

» **MOBILE CORPS:** The mirror image of an armor corps, a mobile corps emphasizes speed with three mobile battlegroups and one armor battlegroup.

AS IT ADVANCES ACROSS AN ENEMY CITY, AN IMPERIAL ARMOR CORPS LEAVES RUBBLE IN ITS PATH.

ARMY

STRUCTURE: Four corps
COMMANDER'S RANK: General
CAPABLE OF: Capturing a system

An army, composed of four corps, is considered the minimum unit for holding a key planetary system.

» **SYSTEMS ARMY:** Comprised of one to three armies and their supporting elements, a systems army may be deployed across one or more star systems.

» **SECTOR ARMY:** Several systems armies operating within a star sector are referred to as a sector army. Due to the political complications of sector administration, a sector army is sometimes answerable to the decisions of the local Moff.

GUERILLA EFFORTS WON'T BE ENOUGH TO DISLODGE THE IMPERIAL ARMY FROM THE CORE SYSTEMS. —WEEKAN

Important Organizational Distinctions of the Imperial Army

» **ARMY COMMAND:** Senior generals who oversee all aspects of the Imperial Army and who report to Military High Command

» **ASSAULT ARMOR DIVISION:** Encompasses all mechanized war vehicles including walkers, repulsor vehicles, and tanks

» **IMPERIAL MARITIME DIVISION:** Operates on oceans, rivers, and urban waterways utilizing specialized aquatic vehicles such as destroyers, submersibles, and waveskimmers

» **GROUND SUPPORT WING:** Support fighter craft, such as garrison-based TIE fighters not operated by the Imperial Navy

VEHICLES OF THE IMPERIAL ARMY

By Colonel Maximilian Veers

IMPERIAL WALKERS

The Thundering Herd. The Whelmer Stampede. The Black Banthas. In the Imperial Army, mechanized infantry and heavy armor comes with the sound of stomping feet. Enemies of the Empire are ground into the dirt beneath us. These are our walkers. Understand and respect them.

Walkers have advantages over treaded and repulsorlift vehicles, evidenced by their designation as all terrain. Walkers can react to changing surface conditions and shift their footing as a soldier would. Yet they remain firmly connected to the ground to brace against the recoil of their heavy weapons. Walkers can operate freely when atmospheric conditions—such as those on Jabiim or Drongar—prohibit the operation of repulsorlifts. They are immune to anti-repulsorlift jammers.

However, not every walker is appropriate for every environment, and the Imperial Army does not settle for the lowest common denominator. Our walker variants cover every possible need.

WALKERS: ARMORED ASSAULT
All Terrain Armored Transport
(AT-AT)

The pride of the Imperial Assault Armor Division, the quadrupedal AT-AT stands 22.5 meters and is recognized as a symbol of intense power. The AT-AT has a potent effect on primitive Rimmers who see it as a gargantuan beast, as well as galactic citizens trained by propaganda to believe the appearance of an AT-AT means all is lost.

A commander must remember AT-ATs, aside from their symbolic function, are troop transports, and are not as heavily armed as other walkers in the Imperial Army. Two fire-linked heavy laser cannons are mounted on the chin, and two variable-elevation medium repeating blasters are mounted on either side of the head. AT-ATs do not have rear-facing weaponry. To compensate for their blind spots, AT-ATs must be deployed in staggered formations and accompanied by support vehicles.

The AT-AT carries up to forty troopers and five speeder bikes, as well as

But not immune to explosive mines. A walker won't get far with one of its feet blown off. —MADINE

Psychological destabilization. The Alliance can't use these vehicles. We stand for hope, not fear. —Mothma

REBELS ARE LIKE RATS, SKULKING UNDERFOOT AND WAITING TO BITE. ON THE BATTLEFIELD, DESTROY POCKETS OF COVER WITH THE AT-AT'S CHIN GUNS.

modular heavy weaponry to be assembled on site. Troopers disembark by rappelling to the surface.

The command cockpit is located within the AT-AT's head, and is manned by a crew of three: a pilot, a gunner, and a commander. The AT-AT can reach speeds of 60 km/hr, and each footfall echoes with a tremor that is felt long before the walker itself looms into view.

Planetary garrisons modify their AT-ATs to suit the local environments with additions such as gas filters, heat recirculators, and anti-corrosive sheens. Extreme modifications executed by the garrison on Kabaira resulted in the so-called AT-AT Swimmer, a design later produced as the Aquatic Terrain Armored Transport.

AT-AT SWIMMERS CURRENTLY BLOCKING OUR ADVANCES ON KAAL. RECOMMEND IMPORTING ATTACK SUBS FROM MON CALA. —RIEEKAN

REPORT:

UNDERSTANDING AND PREPARING FOR ENEMY EXPLOITATION OF AT-AT VULNERABILITIES

By Captain Nyrox, Raithal Academy

The AT-AT is the workhorse of the Imperial Army, offering a superior balance of firepower, protection, and mobility. However the method by which it achieves that mobility, its legs, leave it vulnerable if an AT-AT commander is unprepared for specific vectors of attack.

◊ High center of gravity can lead to tripping. AT-ATs do not regain their footing easily. Crumbling terrain can unbalance the vehicle.

◊ Damage to knee joints can lead to loss of mobility. Because they represent the flexible joining of two components, the walker's joints are less sound than the other parts of the leg.

◊ Puncturing of the flexible neck section can lead to a reactor breach. Although the scenario is unlikely, it is potentially catastrophic.

POSITION WALKER TO AVOID ENEMY EXPOSURE TO NECK SECTION *Try harpoons and tow cables. That's a good trick. —Wedge*

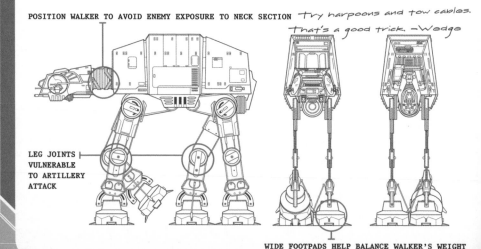

LEG JOINTS VULNERABLE TO ARTILLERY ATTACK

WIDE FOOTPADS HELP BALANCE WALKER'S WEIGHT

All Terrain Tactical Enforcer (AT-TE)

As the first walker to see extensive combat under modern battlefield conditions, the AT-TE brought countless worlds to heel during the Clone Wars. The AT-TE is essentially the predecessor to the Imperial Army's current array of walkers, and is so well built that many remain in active use throughout the Mid and Outer Rim.

Both an assault vehicle and a transport, the AT-TE can deploy its twenty troopers from a rear-mounted staging ramp. It is operated by a crew of seven: one pilot, one spotter, four gunners, and one cannon operator. Its top-mounted mass-driver cannon can fire bunker-buster explosive charges, but it has a slow rate of fire. The sides of the AT-TE bristle with six smaller laser cannons, each positioned so the walker's gunners can fire down upon infantry to stem the advancement of an enemy.

The six legs and low center of gravity give the AT-TE stability and provide a top speed of 60 km/hr. Magnetized footpads allow the AT-TE to scale vertical surfaces or to cling to asteroid surfaces and ship hulls in extraplanetary environments. On Rim worlds, AT-TEs are utilized as patrol vehicles, painted in local camouflage and outfitted with modifications such as floodlights, underbrush grinders, and flamethrowers.

WALKERS: HEAVY CAVALRY
All Terrain Scout Transport (AT-ST)

The bipedal scout walker is a lightly armored, agile ground unit operated by a crew of two. At 8.6 meters in height, the AT-ST can reach speeds of up to 90 km/hr. Its maneuverability and speed make it ideal for tight urban confines.

The AT-ST has a double blaster cannon mounted on its chin as well as a concussion grenade launcher and a blaster cannon mounted on its head. These weapons make the AT-ST effective at targeting armored vehicles. Its feet feature jutting durasteel claws for slicing through enemy barricades. It also possesses a gyroscopic balance system to help it maintain its footing.

Variants of the AT-ST include the Construction Transport (AT-CT), which features repulsor beams for hefting objects, and the Missile Platform (AT-MP), which features multiple missile launchers and a rotary chaingun.

AN AT-PT'S MISSILE LAUNCHER IS DEVASTATING AGAINST INFANTRY.

All Terrain Personal Transport (AT-PT)

As is evident by its designation, the AT-PT is operated by a single trooper. It turns a soldier into an armored, elevated weapons platform, and adds extra firepower to a standard infantry formation.

Measuring 3 meters in height, an AT-PT can reach speeds of 60 km/hr. It is not typically used in a reconnaissance or hit-and-fade capacity. Its armor can withstand small-arms fire but not the heavier punch of anti-vehicle weapons. AT-PTs generally support infantry and should never be expected to take a fortification on their own.

Against enemy troopers or civilian rioters, an AT-PT can dole out impressive damage. Each AT-PT is equipped with twin blaster cannons and a concussion grenade launcher, perfect for shredding tightly packed formations.

All Terrain Recon Transport (AT-RT)

The AT-RT, or recon walker, is a two-legged, single-pilot vehicle used for reconnaissance, minor skirmishes, and picket patrols. While in use since the Clone Wars, the AT-RT is still preferred over the 74-Z speeder bike by several notable scouting units

Commonly used in police units, too. Easy to steal on most Rim worlds. —MADINE

THE AT-RT CAN LEAP OVER GAPS AND BARRIERS.

including Lightning Squadron of the 91st Mobile Reconnaissance Corps.

Standing 3.2 meters tall, the AT-RT can reach speeds up to 90 km/hr and can leap across large gaps. Although its open cockpit design exposes the pilot to hostile fire, it is a necessary trade-off for lightweight construction and mobility. The AT-RT is armed with a repeating blaster cannon that is effective against infantry, and a mortar launcher for long-range strikes on enemy emplacements.

All Terrain Defense Pod (AT-DP)

This variant of the AT-ST has a low-set, heavily armored head with a single laser cannon mounted beneath its chin. The blisters on the right and left sides of the cockpit have narrow slits that allow crewmembers to fire at flanking threats. AT-DPs are deployed as police vehicles on worlds where rebel unrest seems probable.

WALKERS: ARTILLERY
All Terrain Anti-Aircraft (AT-AA)

Always pointing toward the skies, the four-legged AT-AA is invaluable for providing cover against enemy strafing runs that might otherwise decimate an infantry formation. The AT-AA is operated by a three-member crew: one pilot and two gunners. Its top-mounted flak pod or rocket launcher has a 360-degree rotation to track airborne targets and bring them down with fire shrapnel canisters and homing missiles.

The AT-AA is especially deadly when matched against low-flying airspeeders, such as the T-47s favored by the Rebel Alliance. But it lacks anti-personnel weapons. In cases where an AT-AA has stood alone against advancing enemy troops, the crew has been known to fire their rifles through the walker's hatches.

THE AT-DP IS BEST USED FOR PATROL AND POLICING MISSIONS.

THE SPHA-T IS NOT SPEEDY. IF YOU ARE FORCED TO RETREAT, THE ENEMY MAY OVERRUN YOUR ARTILLERY LINE.

Self-Propelled Heavy Artillery (SPHA)

The SPHA is a large, slow-moving artillery vehicle with legs. While shelling long-range targets it must remain stationary, therefore its twelve legs are used only when maneuvering between firing positions. Each SPHA is operated by a crew of thirty, including troopers who secure the perimeter against enemy attack during the vulnerable process of deployment and firing.

The SPHA is modular, meaning its main gun can be swapped out for specialized weaponry. Common variants in active Imperial service include:

» **TURBOLASER (SPHA-T):** A direct line-of-sight turbolaser cannon, which produces a single destructive beam formed from several smaller beams

» **ION CANNON (SPHA-I):** A direct line-of-sight ion cannon used to scramble the electronic systems of vehicles and airspeeders

» **CONCUSSION MISSILE (SPHA-C):** A high-angle parabolic missile launcher

» **MASS DRIVER (SPHA-M):** A high-angle parabolic launcher which fires a projectile that releases an intense kinetic energy at the point of impact

» **THERMOBARIC BURST (SPHA-F):** A high-angle parabolic launcher, which discharges a projectile that ignites the surrounding atmosphere at the point of impact and generates a brief but apocalyptic firestorm

I don't care if it's a thermobaric burst or a superlaser. Indiscriminate military tactics are indefensible.

Leia

IMPERIAL MECHANIZED AND REPULSORLIFT UNITS

Imperial armored and heavy cavalry ground vehicles are not limited to walkers. Treaded, wheeled, and repulsorlift units fill a number of front-line roles, from direct fire to reconnaissance. Vehicles capable of carrying troopers into battle serve as mechanized infantry and provide fire support for those troopers after arrival. Light repulsorlift units, such as speeder bikes, are often used to support expeditionary forces.

MECHANIZED: ARMORED ASSAULT
HAVw A6 Juggernaut

This turbo tank is a heavy assault vehicle birthed in the fires of the Clone Wars. Unlike walkers or repulsortanks, the Juggernaut uses a wheeled configuration and can carry up to 300 troopers. At 30 meters tall and 50 meters long, the Juggernaut presents a large target. However with a turret-mounted heavy laser cannon, a rapid repeating laser cannon, four medium antipersonnel cannons, and two turret-mounted concussion missile launchers, it is equipped to respond to threats.

The Juggernaut has an infamously thick shell made from thermally ablative durasteel armor. Its weight and size can cause issues in certain terrain, but on level surfaces the Juggernaut can reach speeds of 160 km/hr. Limited lateral movement and a wide turning radius make the Juggernaut best suited for straight-line assaults on enemy barricades.

While the main hull of this vehicle can withstand immense fire, the lookout tower atop the vehicle presents an obvious target. The trooper assigned to the lookout tower should be prepared to draw hostile fire. This predictable enemy behavior has been nicknamed "lighting up the lighthouse."

Imperial-class 1-H repulsortank

This mainstay of the Imperial Army since its inception is the signature vehicle of the 112th Repulsorlift Armor Regiment, or the Hell's Hammers. The 1-H repulsortank sports a standard-issue heavy laser cannon as well as a medium blaster cannon. Two additional blaster cannons mounted on either side augment what is already a formidable amount of firepower in a compact profile. Be aware of the fact that atmospheric interference or repulsorlift jammers can render repulsortanks grounded.

A single Juggernaut can operate as an unassailable mobile command center, unless it breaks down. Fortunately this happens all the time. —MADINE

THE ALLIANCE DOESN'T HAVE THE RESOURCES TO FIELD REPULSORLIFT JAMMERS. IN FACT I'M SURPRISED THE EMPIRE ISN'T REGULARLY DEPLOYING THEM AGAINST US. —RIEEKAN

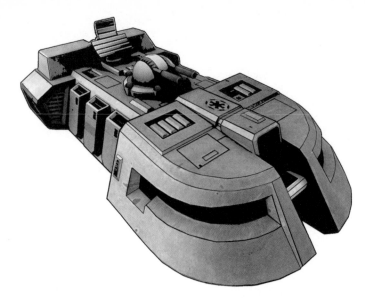

A TROOP TRANSPORT IS ARMORED AND CAPABLE OF REACHING HIGH SPEEDS. DON'T HESITATE TO RAM AN ENEMY POSITION.

Imperial troop transport

This armored speeder is a mainstay of any planetary occupation. It requires a minimum crew of three—a driver, a forward gunner, and a turret gunner—and can comfortably carry ten troopers. An ambushed transport has the ability to fight back with its two forward-mounted laser cannons and its twin blaster turret, while six open-air passenger pockets (three to a side) provide cover for troopers as they return fire with their blaster rifles. Any captured rebels can fit with immobilization hoods for transport to the nearest Imperial garrison.

MECHANIZED: HEAVY AND LIGHT CAVALRY
Century Tank

While the Navy may boast of their TIEs, the Imperial Army's TIEs are superior. The century tank, commonly known as the TIE Crawler, is a compact assault vehicle propelled by twin treads and operated by a single driver. The century tank can reach speeds of 90 km/hr and is often used as fire support for infantry. It is armed with a pair of medium blaster cannons on the forward cockpit and a retractable light turbolaser mounted underneath. The century tank is the pride of the 71st Elite Mechanized Assault Group.

The vehicle's components are modular, thus, in addition to keeping costs low, this innovation allows a commander to field many century tanks at once. The parts are sourced from Santhe/Sienar Technologies, which is why they bear the familiar round cockpit of the TIE fighter.

74-Z Speeder Bike

The 74-Z is the primary repulsorlift craft operated by Imperial scouts. Lightweight and maneuverable, the 74-Z is <u>stripped down</u> to its fundamentals for enhanced speed. To that end armament is scaled back to reduce weight, giving the 74-Z a single, forward-facing blaster cannon mounted on the undercarriage.

With its simple controls and minimalist frame, the repulsorlift engine can push speeds over 500 km/hr. At those speeds, it has been rumored that the 74-Z is "unsafe in any atmosphere" and a "death trap." However, the 74-Z's terrain-following sensors link up to the visual HUD inside its driver's helmet giving the trooper perfect vision of what lies ahead and putting to rest the defamatory rumors.

BARC Speeder

Reliable even after decades of use, the Biker Advanced Recon Commando (BARC) was produced in the millions during the Clone Wars for military and police duty. The Imperial Army later claimed the BARC for reconnaissance and hit-and-fade missions carried out by its scout units. Even today, many scouting units operate with BARCs despite institutional pressure to adopt the nimbler 74-Zs.

The advantage of the BARC, and why it has found a home with so many planetary police forces, is that it rarely needs maintenance and never seems to show damage. Equipped with a turbine engine, two blaster cannons on the nose and two more at the rear, the BARC is as well-armed as it is fast, with most drivers operating at speeds in the 400 km/hr range.

An engine and a steering vane. Even i don't like to operate these things, and people say i'm a good pilot. —Wedge

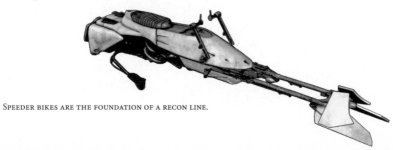

SPEEDER BIKES ARE THE FOUNDATION OF A RECON LINE.

IMPERIAL GARRISONS

A protracted campaign or a planetary occupation requires a base of operations.

An Imperial Army commander can achieve maximum psychological impact by turning a venerated political or religious structure into the Imperial seat of power, but such a structure may not be optimized for defense. The prefabricated Imperial garrison solves this problem.

The manufacturing contract for Imperial garrisons has been awarded to Rothana Heavy Engineering. The following pages include the company's official statement on design and specifications.

An Imperial garrison is elevated for observation, angled for defense, and a symbol to rebellious populations that the Empire isn't going anywhere.

IM-455 MODULAR GARRISON: THE PEACEKEEPER

"Their pacification is your security"

Greetings! As the commander of an IM-455 modular garrison you are in possession of an impregnable fortress that stands as a symbol of Imperial power.

LAYOUT

The IM-455 follows a consistent structural configuration:

- **Levels 1–5:** Vehicle bays (large enough to accommodate AT-AT walkers), troop quarters, a detention block, an armory, a medbay, and a recreation center (we have recently added a scoopball court by popular request)

- **Level 6:** Officers' quarters, pilots' quarters, monitoring stations, and command headquarters

- **Level 7:** TIE fighter hangars

- **Level 8:** Launch chutes for TIE fighters and control rooms for TIE ground crew members

- **Roof:** Sensor suite tower, equipped with a hypercom array and Rothana's patented mix of thermo-infra-ecto multivariate sensors

> **NOTE:** Main reactor is buried safely underground

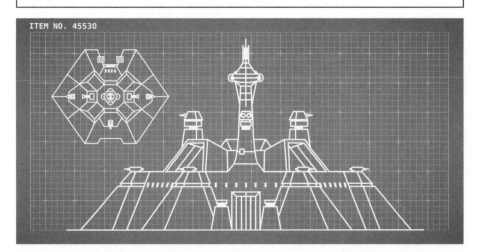

ITEM NO. 45530

Chewie and I got ourselves inside these things more than once.
Madine—send the new recruits my way if they want to learn how it's done.
—Han

Solo . . . if I'd wanted fiction I'd have borrowed a holothriller. —MADINE

PERSONNEL AND EQUIPMENT

The IM-455 can house:

- Up to 3,000 troops and support staff, flexible to your mission needs. Equipped to accommodate technicians, medics, gunners, troopers, AT-AT drivers, mechanics, technicians, and officers.
- 10 AT-ATs.
- 10 AT-STs.
- 50–100 speeder bikes or landspeeders.
- 36–40 TIE fighters (three squadrons).

DEFENSES AND ARMAMENT

The IM-455 comes complete with:

- 3 twin turbolasers, turret-mounted for maximum field-of-fire coverage.
- 6 heavy laser turrets.
- 6 tractor beam projectors.
- 2 directional EMP pulse generators.
- 48 anti-infantry blaster cannons.
- A variable ray- and particle-shield generator. to withstand orbital bombardment or hostile artillery.
- Full-perimeter (10-meter) shredder fencing, lethally electrified.
- Guard towers every 100 meters equipped with floodlights and emergency alarms.
- 720 HX7 antipersonnel mines, to be placed around the garrison's perimeter after installation.

Brings to mind the smell of singed Wookiee hair. Occupational hazard in my line of work. —Han

---

NOTE: Rumors that a single bounty hunter recently breached an Imperial garrison are completely false. Nevertheless, if you are interested in purchasing our newest defensive upgrade (XZD-001: FETT COUNTERMEASURES), please contact your Rothana representative.

ITEM NOS. 55530-39, 897, 401

IM-8005 SHIELD PROJECTOR GARRISON: THE SHARPLENS
"Security that keeps an eye on the sky"

With the rise of Imperial orbital construction projects, Rothana has rolled out a new line of garrisons. The IM-8005 projects an uninterrupted energy shield around the orbital site, and is simultaneously equipped to put down planetside uprisings from the conscripted workforce.

Full specifications are available upon request, but key elements of the IM-8005 include:

- **Landing pad:** 20 meters tall to accommodate docking AT-ATs. Sufficient surface area to accommodate two to three *Lambda*-class shuttles.

- **Command garrison:** Similar to the IM-455 but broken into several smaller structures. Due to the considerable power requirements of the shield generator, the IM-8005's main reactor is held within an armored bunker.

- **Shield generator:** The most prominent feature of the IM-8005 is its SLD-26 planetary shield generator. Its dish projects an energy sphere at a distance of up to 2,600 kilometers, completely enveloping its target with overlapping ray and energy shields. If you are concerned about potential sabotage to the focusing dish or other prominent features, a Rothana representative would be happy to discuss options for upgrading your defensive systems.

ALSO AVAILABLE FROM ROTHANA:

Rogue Squadron just returned from Ootoola. Apparently these things have a blind spot around their equators. Scratch one Hexostar. —Wedge

IM-S-653 ORBITAL GARRISON: THE HEXOSTAR

Our most cost-efficient solution! The Hexostar is formed from two surface garrisons joined together at the base, positioned in orbit where it can easily track and eliminate any surface or space-based target.

ITEM NO. 49980

IM-X-981 HOSTILE-ENVIRONMENT GARRISON: THE PURITY

This deluxe garrison model includes radiation shielding and space-rated airlocks. Don't let something as predictable as the weather get in the way of dispensing justice.

ITEM NO. 48320

IM-A-761 OCEANIC GARRISON: THE BLACKFATHOM

Repulsorlifts keep this model afloat and stable even during the heaviest waves. This feature is now guaranteed following the NewsNet frenzy surrounding the incident on Shaum Hii. Underwater hangar bays allow the IM-A-761 to deploy its fleet of repulsor-subs and AT-AT Swimmers.

ITEM NO. 48002

MOUNTED CREATURES

MOUNTED CREATURES

As a base commander, how many times has this happened to you? The harsh conditions found in the local environment debilitate your mechanized scout vehicles, keeping them shut in the repair bays for weeks.

To ease your headaches, Rothana is happy to offer all Imperial base commanders the option to purchase environmentally appropriate mounts and pack animals. Keep your garrison humming amidst the severest environments!

DEWBACKS

These scaly quadrupeds originally hail from desert climes. While dewbacks will eat almost anything, they do spit. (NOTE: due to ectothermic thermophysiology, we do not ship dewbacks to locations where the local temperature is below the freezing point of water.)

16,000 credits for a herd of six

GETTING A STUBBORN DEWBACK TO MOVE IS AS HOPELESS AS SHOVELING A SAND DUNE. I DOUBT EVEN THE EMPIRE CAN MAKE IT HAPPEN. —LUKE

AIWHAS

If you've got the operational budget, we've got the mount! Take to the skies with the aiwha, a natural flyer that can also swim through shallow water. For any world with a breathable atmosphere, aiwhas are the perfect mount. Perform reconnaissance from 5,000 meters overhead, or travel between two Imperial outposts with no trail or terrain worries.

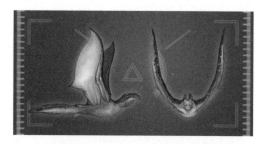

45,000 credits a head (starting price)
Large, cargo-hauling breeds available
under the premium pricing model

GELAGRUBS

Gelatinous ground beetles, plucked directly from the hothouse jungles of Felucia, are slow and sticky but sure-footed even on steep inclines. Our custom, genetically stunted gelagrubs are guaranteed not to pupate into beetles! They eat an exclusive diet of mushrooms and similar fungi. No fungus? No problem! Rothana offers freeze-dried packets of specially formulated feed for an additional fee.

Gelagrubs are available by special order only. Please contact your representative for pricing.

CRACIAN THUMPERS

These even-tempered herbivores keep calm under fire and can shoulder heavy loads. Cracian thumpers are born runners and can keep a steady pace for hours—yet they stay whisper-quiet. Perfect for use in scouting an enemy line.

WE'VE USED THUMPERS AT THE BASES ON FANGOL, DANKAYO, AND NISHR. THEY'RE MORE AGREEABLE THAN TAUNTAUNS, I'LL SAY THAT MUCH. —RIEEKAN

2,000 credits a head for common thumper
5,000–7,000 credits a head for specialty breeds

BLURRGS

Exported from a desert world in the Gaulus sector, these hardy, two-legged reptiles are reliable beasts. Though a bit dim, they can be quite noisy when agitated.

12,000 credits for six or package pricing of 20,000 for a herd of twelve

MISSION REPORT: THE PACIFICATION OF SALLINE

The Importance of Unit Support in Armored Assault

By Colonel Maximilian Veers

Chandrila is a jewel of the Core Worlds but has historically harbored factions of dissent and treason. When the Rebel Alliance seized the port city of Salline, the Empire had to move quickly to remove the infestation.

While AT-ATs would be the natural choice as primary combat vehicles for the Salline operation, no one wanted a repeat of the debacle on Ord Torrenze. There, as a single AT-AT marched through a dense urban center to eliminate a safehouse, rebels fired from building windows after the walker's head (and its four laser cannons) had passed. Although AT-ATs are built to withstand a certain amount of blaster fire, the vehicle on Ord Torrenze eventually succumbed to the sustained barrage. The resulting loss cost the Empire three officers, forty stormtroopers, five crew members, and military equipment valued at more than 13 million credits.

Charged with bringing Salline into line, I requested two AT-ATs (Hammer 6 and Hammer 8) to provide direct fire, and four AT-STs to provide fire support. Dropships from the Star Destroyer *Viscount* put us into position and we advanced on Salline at 0200 as Chandrila's sun rose at our backs. Rebels had fortified the government center on the coast, but all of downtown Salline had been designated a free-fire zone.

I placed Hammer 6 on point and followed in Hammer 8 at a distance of 200 meters. Two AT-STs accompanied each of us to cover our flanks. We proceeded down Guildhead's Way, a broad avenue that provided an unobstructed path to the government center.

Hammer 6 came under fire approximately 1.2 kilometers from our objective. Rebels concealed in the upper stories of a building on the south side of Guildhead's Way unloaded missile batteries on Hammer 6 as soon as it passed their position.

Upon seeing the source of the attack, I ordered Hammer 8 to fire on the building with its chin cannons, blowing out the upper stories. The escorting AT-STs eliminated the Rebel survivors as they fled the structure through its ground floor.

This pattern repeated itself another 400 meters farther down the road. However, this time Hammer 6 took a missile to its rear hip, aggravating a preexisting maintenance problem, causing the joint to seize up, and forcing the walker to drag its rear left leg. Though this is not a failure of tactics, I ordered Hammer 6 to remain in position and act as an elevated gun platform, providing 180-degree coverage fire as needed by sweeping its neck.

I brought Hammer 8 up to the lead position and preceded the remainder of the distance to the government center. After Hammer 8 blasted a hole through the security wall and entered the inner courtyard, I gave the surrender order over the loudspeaker.

The vermin fled their rathole before Hammer 8's stormtroopers could rappel to the ground and charge the building. Several high-speed watercraft sped away from the nearby docks and streaked across the ocean. Though I could not pursue, I contacted the *Viscount* to request a flight of TIE fighters. The TIEs intercepted the fleeing Rebels seven kilometers south of Salline and blasted their boats from the water.

PART IV

THE STORMTROOPER CORPS

By TX-5532

Stormtroopers are the knife's edge.

We are the first to go in. We face the enemy when they are strongest. We do not stop until we have achieved our objective. The Imperial Army walks in the path we blaze.

We are independent, but complete joint operations with other branches of the military service. With the Imperial Navy, we serve aboard their warships and execute boarding operations against hostile vessels. With the Imperial Army, we seize starports and take out gun emplacements.

The Stormtrooper Corps is unconcerned with long-term occupation. We are deployed when our Emperor requires our service and are recalled when he needs us elsewhere. The Stormtrooper Corps is streamlined and ready for rapid deployment. We operate on every planet in the Empire, and thus, the white helmet we don is the face of the Imperial military.

The tighter the helmet, the dumber the trooper. —Han

We are stormtroopers, distinguished by a heritage of physical perfection and an unshakable ideology. If we are fewer in number than the assembled ranks of the Army and Navy, that is just as it should be. The narrower the blade, the sharper the edge.

THE STORMTROOPER CORPS IS ONLY AS STRONG AS ITS SOLDIERS.

HISTORY OF THE STORMTROOPER CORPS

The Stormtrooper Corps is unparalleled. Do not compare us to the feeble Judicial Security forces that existed in the dying decades of the Old Republic. You must look back nearly four thousand years to the time of Republic rocket-jumpers to find an equivalent corps of elite, first-attack soldiers. Perhaps inspired by the military glories of previous millennia, our wise Emperor authorized the deployment of millions of Kamino-grown clone troopers to put an end to the Separatist crisis.

That was the Clone Wars. The clone troopers, through genetics and training, possessed martial strength that no Separatist droid could match. They outclassed their ostensible commanders, the Jedi Knights. Under the corrupt political system of the Old Republic, the clone troopers were forced to take orders from sword-carrying pacifists who had no business play-acting as military tacticians. When the Jedi showed their true colors with an assassination plot against Supreme Chancellor Palpatine, it was the clone troopers who put down the Jedi uprising.

From those elite, veteran clone troopers, the nucleus of the Emperor's new Stormtrooper Corps was formed. Under this proud banner, they continued to fight against Separatist holdouts and radicals who resisted the New Order.

Yes, the clone troopers had done their job, but it was a role they'd been bred for. Even more remarkable was the swell of young patriots who volunteered to follow their example. As the Imperial military expanded, the Stormtrooper Corps diversified. Our ranks soon included snowtroopers, sandtroopers, scout troopers, and more. These brave men and women survived our training crucibles and proved themselves worthy of being called Imperial stormtroopers. Unified under a single cause, behind a common mask, each trooper makes a pledge.

I am a stormtrooper. My skin is my armor. My face is my helmet. My name is my number. I am fulfilled, for I am an agent of the Emperor.

No. I was there. Palpatine may think he can write his own history, but he cannot erase my memories. —Mothma

CLONING AND RECRUITMENT

By Nala Se,
Quality Control, Tipoca City, Kamino

First-Gen Clones

Much misinformation exists. To set the record straight for commanders like yourself, who may be called upon to lead clone soldiers or commission new batches, Kaminoan geneticists are the best in the galaxy. The clones produced for the Grand Army of the Republic were nearly flawless. Those clones were bred for warfare and were unflinching under fire. The reports of anomalous behaviors on Christophsis and Ringo Vinda are not only statistically insignificant, but most likely the result of Jedi tampering. The desire to diversify the genetic stock is understandable, but there is no reason to cancel future orders of this specific model.

FIRST-GEN DETAILS: Genetic Template

TEMPLATE: Jango Fett

BIRTH: Concord Dawn

DEATH: Geonosis

AGE AT TIME OF DEATH: 44 standard years

OCCUPATION: Former bounty hunter

NOTABLE GENETIC OFFSPRING (PRODUCED SEPARATELY FROM GAR CLONES): Boba Fett (unit A0050)

Recruitment

Far be it from me to criticize the Empire's policy of welcoming patriotic citizens into the ranks of the Stormtrooper Corps. These less-pricey "natural" recruits are sufficient for the Empire's current needs, but in order to maintain the integrity of the program, optimal morphologic consistency with previous cloning standards is required. Diverse, undirected human genetic stock may be constrained if we adhere to strict standards of conformity. As a cost bonus, this also allows for interchangeable uniforms and armor. If you command these troopers, rest assured they meet the minimum physical benchmarks as Kamino-grown clones.

Current Imperial stormtrooper recruiting requirements:

Genetic suitability vs. clone template (human genome): 97.5% or higher

HEIGHT: 1.79–1.85 m
WEIGHT: 78–85 kg
BODY MASS/MUSCULATURE RATING: Scala scoring of 22.x5 or less
TACTICAL INTELLIGENCE RATING: Marrev testing result of 790 or higher
RECEPTIVITY TO INDOCTRINATION RATING: Minimum Class C

Hey, looks like I qualify. And Luke was wondering why his stormtrooper armor didn't fit. —Han

ACADEMIES AND TRAINING

Elite stormtrooper cadets carry out their training at the Academy of Carida. The facilities there produce superior stormtrooper officers. Those who survive their years at Cliffside on Carida earn the right to lead their fellow stormtroopers.

At Carida, stormtrooper officer candidates undergo:

» Wilderness survival
» Desert warfare simulation
» Underwater battle tactics
» Experimental weapons testing
» Flash-memory instruction in military history
» Self-discipline through emotional suppression
» Education in the principles of the Emperor's New Order

RECRUITMENT

The Empire's many victories against the forces of rebellion and chaos have inspired common Imperial citizens to ask how they may serve the Emperor. As a result of what they have witnessed on the Imperial NewsNets, many seek to wear the polished white armor of the Stormtrooper Corps.

The Sunstorm entrance of the Carida Academy

Only a few succeed. Most fail to meet the posted physical requirements. Others wash out during training. Passing the merciless standards of the Stormtrooper Corps is a point of honor for those within our ranks, but the unfit need not despair. The Imperial Army and Navy need recruits too.

Imperial recruiters actively seek those who desire a career of service and are willing to die for a cause. We are stormtroopers; we believe in our Emperor.

IMPERIAL RECRUITERS ARE ON THE LOOKOUT FOR PROMISING CANDIDATES AND WELCOME YOUR RECOMMENDATIONS.

The Alliance must recruit Carida or contain it as part of our long term plan for weakening the Empire's military infrastructure. —Mothma

VERY LONG TERM, I'M AFRAID. RECRUITING CARIDA IS OUT OF THE QUESTION. CONTAINING IT? DIFFICULT BUT POSSIBLE. WE WILL NEVER CONQUER CARIDA. —RIEEKAN

THE IMPERIAL STORMTROOPER

Stormtrooper ideology is terrifying in its thoroughness. They can't be reasoned with, which means they can't be deprogrammed. —Leia

A stormtrooper is a select warrior. He cannot be bribed or blackmailed. He is unswerving in his obedience and unflinching in his dispensation of Imperial justice.

Stormtroopers are victorious because of our training, our uniformity, and our ability to bring overwhelming firepower to bear. We offer our lives for our Emperor.

STORMTROOPER ARMOR

Basic Imperial stormtrooper armor is derived from what was worn by the clone troopers at the Battle of Geonosis in the Clone Wars.

The armor is made from an energy-diffusing and impact-resistant plastoid. When assembled, the eighteen-piece suit covers a trooper from head to toe in a protective shell.

Rank-and-file stormtroopers look identical to outsiders. An individual trooper can identify his squadmates with IFF transponder readouts displayed within his helmet. General citizens and our foes see only a united and implacable face. When enemies witness a stormtrooper fall only to

watch a duplicate take his place, they lose the will to fight.

However, it is the responsibility of an officer to know the soldiers behind the helmet. Understanding the armor will help you understand the trooper.

1. BLACK BODY GLOVE. This flexible garment provides insulation and cushioning while also regulating body temperature during exertion. If a stormtrooper is injured, it acts as a compression sleeve to stem bleeding. It will also maintain cellular integrity in the event of a catastrophic reactor leak.

2. LEG SEGMENTS. There are two segments per leg. The lower-right leg segment contains auxiliary power cells. The lower-left segment has a reinforced ridge over the knee area to protect the exposed joint when firing from a kneeling position. Due to recruiting and rigorous conditioning, all stormtroopers favor their right side and adopt identical kneeling positions.

3. TORSO SECTION. The chestpiece offers the greatest protection from

How to put holes in the bucketheads: stormtrooper weak points include the gap between the chestplate and the shoulder armor. Plus any approach that puts you in the wind spot of the trooper's peripheral vision. Their helmet sensors aren't nearly as good as they claim. —Wedge

shrapnel, projectiles, flames, and corrosives. Hits from blasters and other handheld energy weapons will disperse across the surface area of the armor's plasteel, however, close-range impacts will penetrate. Manual controls located on the lower torso section allow the trooper to adjust the environmental regulation of the integrated armor and body glove.

4. ARM SEGMENTS. Forearm segments are reinforced to intercept vibroblades during close-quarters combat. With an optional modification, the gloves can deliver stun shocks.

5. HELMET. The stormtrooper helmet is made of the same plastoid composite as the rest of the armor, but it incorporates an inner layer of magnetic shielding. Filters within the helmet screen out chemical and biological contaminants, while heat dispersal vents maintain a consistent temperature. Polarized lenses collect non-visual data for display on the helmet's holographic HUD visual. The lenses adjust for environmental conditions, such as automatically darkening to prevent retinal damage from explosions.

Auditory sensors can record and play back sounds. The processed tone of stormtrooper speech is a function of the chin-mounted vocoder. NOTE: The threat-targeting features of a stormtrooper helmet only activate when worn by the helmet's designated trooper. This prevents the helmets from being used by our enemies and reduces their value on the black market.

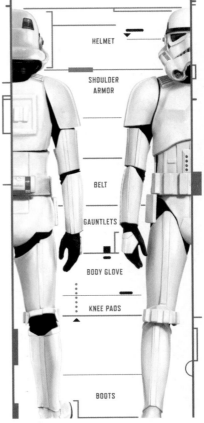

HELMET

SHOULDER ARMOR

BELT

GAUNTLETS

BODY GLOVE

KNEE PADS

BOOTS

Don't pick up an abandoned stormtrooper helmet if a Wookiee recently passed that way. There might still be a head inside it. —Han

STORMTROOPER OFFICERS

Stormtrooper officers can be products of the academy system or troopers promoted from within the ranks. When out of their armor, officers are designated by all-black tunics, trousers, officer's caps, and rank cylinders.

In the field, stormtrooper officers are marked by orange shoulder pauldrons and bear specific rank insignia.

The armor of stormtrooper commanders is also marked, but with blue pauldrons. High-value commanders are provided a personal energy shield for use during combat.

STORMTROOPER OFFICER
(DUTY UNIFORM)

STORMTROOPER OFFICER
(ARMOR)

STORMTROOPER OFFICER
(UNIT MARKINGS)

STORMTROOPER EQUIPMENT

The stormtrooper's removable belt is standard issue, but the equipment carried on it varies depending on mission parameters. Common items include:

» Grappling hook with extendible cable
» C1 military comlink hardwired against jamming
» Clip for attaching the E-11 rifle
» Blaster power packs for the E-11 rifle
» Wrist binders for capturing prisoners
» Survival kit that includes emergency rations, flares, and a medpac
» Electronic lock scrambler/descrambler

Additional equipment is held within the back plating of stormtrooper armor. These items include:

» **PRESSURIZED AIR SUPPLY:** A volume of emergency air that permits a stormtrooper to survive for up to twenty minutes in vacuum

» **POWER PACK:** Rechargeable cells that feed energy to the armor's electronic components (240 hours per standard charge)

» **ENCRYPTED TELEMETRY TRANSMITTER:** A small imbedded disc that allows troopers to identify friend from foe amidst identical armored stormtroopers

Seems like we could have some fun with this if we could figure out a way to jam or spoof the telemetry. Possible project for Drayson? —MADINE

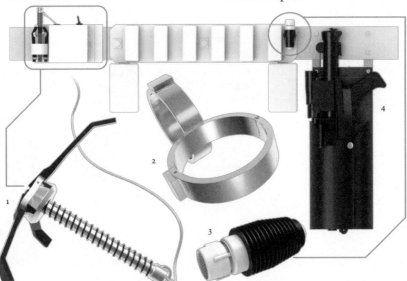

1. Grappling hook; 2. Wrist binders; 3. Comlink; 4. Blaster and holster

STORMTROOPER ARMAMENT BLASTER RIFLE (BLASTECH E-11)

All stormtroopers carry the BlasTech E-11. This is a lightweight, reliable, and accurate blaster rifle with variable settings that range from single fire to fully automatic. Technical stats:

RANGE: 300 meters

NOTE: It is best suited for close-quarters firefights, particularly the narrow confines of enemy installations and starship corridors.

SETTINGS: Stun or kill

AMMUNITION: Blaster packs with power for 500 shots loaded into the side

WEIGHT: 2.6 kg

FEATURE: Optical scope with 2x magnification that interfaces with the tactical HUD within a stormtrooper's helmet

FUNCTION: With stock fully extended, it can be braced against a stormtrooper's shoulder to contain recoil. With stock folded, it has a compact profile and can be carried in one hand.

MAINTENANCE: Regular cleaning and application of anti-corrosive sealant allows the weapon to operate in a vacuum

MODIFICATIONS: Projectile launcher, including grenades and grappling hooks

They forgot one: E-11 rifles jam if you blink at them twice. —Wedge

I've seen drunken Dralls who shoot straighter than the E-11. —Han

WHEN STORMTROOPERS UNDER YOUR COMMAND HAVE DOWNTIME, IT IS SUGGESTED THEY ENGAGE IN MARKSMANSHIP DRILLS.

EXCERPT FROM THE IMPERIAL STORMTROOPER CORPS FIELD MANUAL

SECTION 32.B.ST57

COMBAT OPERATION OF THE E-11 BLASTER RIFLE

Select an optimal firing position based on available cover, the positions of your squadmates, and the number and dispersion of enemy targets. Obtain an overview of the situation while not exposing yourself to hostile fire. Remain alert. Should the situation change unexpectedly, do not allow yourself to be pinned down.

1. After assuming a stable firing position, press the E-11's stock firmly against the shoulder to contain recoil. Point the E-11's muzzle toward the target and line up the shot using the weapon sights.

2. Apply careful aim and trigger control. Determine the target's range and movement speed.

3. Note that aliens do not always share commonalities with human anatomy. Always aim at the center of mass for maximum stopping power.

4. Fire controlled bursts. Long-range targets require greater precision and a slower rate of fire.

5. Keep firing until the enemy is down.

6. Assess the situation to determine if the threat is contained or if engagement with additional targets is required.

7. Low-value enemy survivors can be executed on the spot. High-value or undetermined enemies should be taken into custody and delivered to Imperial Intelligence.

HEAVY WEAPONS (E-WEB HEAVY REPEATING BLASTER)

The BlasTech E-Web is a powerful repeating blaster capable of penetrating vehicular shielding. It is too large to be carried by a single stormtrooper, but all troopers are trained to deploy, aim, and fire this weapon.

RANGE: Maximum 750 meters
SETTINGS: Anti-infantry and armor-penetrating
AMMUNITION: Energy blasts fed from separate power generator
WEIGHT: 38 kg

FEATURE: Can be transported and assembled for firing in less than a minute, however, its Eksoan Class-4T3 generator can take up to ten minutes to reach full power.

FUNCTION: Operated by two storm-troopers. One trooper fires the E-Web from behind its recoil-cushioning tripod. The other monitors and adjusts the generator's power feed to prevent overheating.

MAINTENANCE: Monthly disassembly, inspection, repair, and reassembly

MODIFICATIONS: High-fire repeater setting, automated sentry turret modification kit

EXPLOSIVES (KEY-LOCKED THERMAL DETONATOR)

A single, cylindrical thermal detonator with a baradium core is located on the lower back of all stormtrooper armor.

RANGE: Blast radius of 5 meters
SETTINGS: Time delay 6–18 seconds
AMMUNITION: Explosive baradium core
WEIGHT: 180 g
FEATURE: Security lockout

FUNCTION: Activation is achieved by first entering a unique access code. Each stormtrooper is issued a code at the start of a mission. The keys on the detonator are unlabeled to prevent enemies from arming the detonator, so stormtroopers must employ pattern memorization.

MAINTENANCE: Regular inspection for imperfections in the outer casing, full replacement of any damaged units

MODIFICATIONS: Magnetic and adhesive outer sleeves

STORMTROOPERS WILL SOMETIMES TRIGGER THIS DETONATOR TO AVOID CAPTURE AND INTERROGATION. AND TO SCORE ONE LAST KILL, PRESUMABLY.
— RIEEKAN

EXCERPT FROM THE IMPERIAL STORMTROOPER CORPS FIELD MANUAL

SECTION 32.B.ST57

COMBAT OPERATION OF THE KEY-LOCKED THERMAL DETONATOR

1. Remove thermal detonator from equipment clip on lower back.

2. Inspect detonator for signs of damage and confirm integrity of baradium core. Do not proceed if in posses- sion of a potentially unstable detonator.

3. Estimate target range.

4. Input time delay.

5. Input activation code.

6. Stand half-facing the target; make a lobbed, overhead throw and in the direction of your target.

7. Take cover from the detonator blast. Immediately follow up with concentrated blaster fire against the target position.

STRUCTURE AND ORGANIZATION

Stormtroopers might be the smallest unit of the Imperial military, but we are a distinct military branch with our own chain of command.

Planetside, civilians often mistake stormtroopers for Imperial Army soldiers. In space, it's common for people to assume we're attached to the Imperial Navy. A stormtrooper will not take offense, but as an officer of the Imperial military you should know better.

Stormtrooper Command governs the military operations of the Stormtrooper Corps. The officers of Stormtrooper Command are subservient to the will of Emperor Palpatine. If the Emperor wishes something to be so, it is the stormtroopers who make it happen.

The members of the Royal Guard belong to the Stormtrooper Corps. They serve the Emperor as his personal bodyguards. As such they exist apart from the traditional chain of command, taking their orders directly from His Imperial Majesty and his honored cabal of advisors.

FORMATIONS AND DEPLOYMENT

Each stormtrooper is a formidable fighting unit in isolation. Grouped together, stormtroopers can accomplish any objective on ground, in air, or in space.

SQUAD

STRUCTURE: 8–10 stormtroopers
COMMANDER'S RANK: Sergeant

NOTE: The squad is the smallest stormtrooper unit typically deployed into a threat situation.

STORMTROOPER AND ROYAL GUARD

EXCERPT FROM THE IMPERIAL STORMTROOPER CORPS FIELD MANUAL

SECTION 682.T.ST88

MAINTAINING SQUAD FORMATION

For flexibility in uncertain battle conditions, split your
squad into two fire teams and organize them into wedge
formations. Position the fire team leader at the tip of
each wedge.

Wedge formations permit maximum firing range in every
direction and allow ready communication between members.
Grouping a squad in this manner is advised for situations
in which the composition or position of an enemy force is
unknown.

PLATOON

STRUCTURE: 4–5 squads
COMMANDER'S RANK: Lieutenant and Sergeant Major

NOTE: Like the squad, the stormtrooper platoon is variable in size.

COMPANY

STRUCTURE: 4 platoons
COMMANDER'S RANK: Captain

NOTE: Tango Company fought during the Lasan Suppression, earning its members the Imperial Medal of Valor.

BATTALION

STRUCTURE: 4 companies
COMMANDER'S RANK: Major

NOTE: A stormtrooper battalion is likely to incorporate many types of specialized stormtrooper units, including incinerator stormtroopers and scout troopers.

REGIMENT

STRUCTURE: 4 battalions
COMMANDER'S RANK: Lieutenant Colonel

NOTE: A stormtrooper regiment is considered sufficient to seize a Class A planetary starport.

LEGION

STRUCTURE: 4 regiments
COMMANDER'S RANK: High Colonel

NOTE: The legion is the largest defined level of organization within the Stormtrooper Corps. It is the approximate equivalent of an Imperial Army battlegroup.

A COMPANY SUPPORTED BY ARMORED INFANTRY

THE 501st LEGION

By Commander Mak Tennar

We are elite warriors who serve the Emperor, but we are proud to call ourselves Vader's Fist. The Imperial Navy and Army are critical in maintaining peace in our glorious Empire. The troopers of the 501st Imperial Legion are more than peacekeepers. We serve the highest rulers in the Empire.

The 501st Legion was formed during the Clone Wars, and earned recognition in the Jedi rebellion that brought an end to that conflict. It was the troopers of the 501st who stormed the Jedi Temple to eliminate the false wizards as they hid inside their government fortress. Members of the 501st are hand-picked by Lord Darth Vader from within the stormtrooper units. Battlefield promotions are awarded to those who earn his respect.

The 501st Legion continues to serve Lord Vader in the current emergency, working toward the day when the Rebels will be put in their place.

I WISH I KNEW MORE ABOUT THIS EVENT. DATA RECORDS HAVE BEEN WIPED. ONLY PRINTED STATEMENTS LIKE THIS ONE REMAIN. —LUKE

STORMTROOPER SPECIALIZATIONS

The Empire contains a vast number of worlds. These planets hang in an airless void, lifeboats bobbing in a dead sea. Yet many of these refuges harbor climates hostile to humans. Using a combination of exceptional training and extraordinary armor, members of the Stormtrooper Corps can subdue any environment.

AQUATIC ASSAULT STORMTROOPERS (SEATROOPERS)

Aquatic assault stormtroopers, or seatroopers, are deployed on oceanic worlds to pacify threats beneath the waves. The armor's air supply lasts over an hour and is resistant to crushing ocean depths. Underwater mobility is aided by flippered boots and a backpack propulsion unit.

Seatroopers are often ferried into battle aboard AT-AT Swimmers. However, they have the authority to commandeer Imperial waveskimmers and other aquatic vessels operated by the Imperial Maritime Division. Each seatrooper carries a modified E-11 blaster rifle that doubles as a speargun.

BOMB SQUAD STORMTROOPERS (BOMBTROOPERS)

Imperial bombtroopers are trained to disarm explosive devices, from anti-tank mines to primitive spring traps. Their specialized armor can withstand controlled explosions and high-velocity shrapnel. The helmet of a bombtrooper includes sensors for detecting the chemical signatures of explosives. In addition, the helmet will automatically enable full muffling mode at the first sign of a detonation to protect its wearer from eye or ear damage. Bomb squad stormtroopers are superior to bomb-disposal droids because they are trained to recover the device intact, producing a valuable prize for Imperial Intelligence.

AQUATIC ASSAULT STORMTROOPER

We have mobilized the Mon Calamari Knights to assist in the Alliance's liberation of aquatic worlds. They are uniquely qualified to defeat a foe like seatroopers. —Mothma

INCINERATOR STORMTROOPERS

Incinerator stormtroopers bear red markings on their armor to indicate their specialty. They carry Oppressor flamethrowers and plasma rifles that release wide-beam spreads capable of exciting molecules to their burning point. Trained to lay down flame and reactive chemicals, incinerator troopers are best used against enemy infantry and to purge local villages. Using only thermobaric canisters and mortar launchers, incinerator stormtroopers brought about the Imperial triumph known as the Ash Ruination of New Plympto.

IMPERIAL MARINES

The stormtroopers of the Imperial Marines provide the Imperial Navy their punch. Imperial Marines are stationed on Star Destroyers and other naval warships and serve as the first wave boarding party on captured starships. After breaching the enemy vessel's hull with a cutting laser and an explosive charge, Imperial Marines execute a shock assault with E-11 blaster rifles, MiniMag PTL missile launchers, smoke pellets, and flash grenades. Imperial Marines are also trained to repel hostiles if a ship's defense is breached.

INCINERATOR STORMTROOPER

HAZARD STORMTROOPERS

Extreme planetary climates are nothing to hazard stormtroopers. Their armor is fully sealed against acidic, electromagnetic, biochemical, and other environmental threats. A three-day air supply enriched with beneficial bacteria circulates throughout their suits. Stormtroopers selected for hazard duty undergo cyborg limb replacement to give them the strength and stamina needed to operate their heavy armor for extended missions. They are armed with concussion rifles and heavy repeating blasters.

MAGMA STORMTROOPERS (LAVATROOPERS)

Specially trained to operate in active geologic vents, magma troopers are

They hit Kashyyyk, too, especially Kepitenochan. I've got a real score to settle with these guys. —Han

117

EXCERPT FROM THE IMPERIAL STORMTROOPER CORPS FIELD MANUAL

SECTION 7782.X.ST08

HAZARD TROOPERS—DEALING WITH A CATASTROPHIC FILTER CONTAMINANT

Your helmet HUD will alert you if an atmospheric contaminant has penetrated the filters of your mask and poses a lethal threat. Nothing atypical should be able to penetrate your suit's sealed environment. If any unusual smells or tastes do infiltrate your suit, adhere to the following procedure for immediate containment.

1. Stop breathing. Close your mouth and eyes.

2. Close your helmet filters manually.

3. Hold down your helmet purge valve and sharply exhale to clear the helmet environment.

4. Alert your squad with one of these three alarms:
   o Squad-only comlink alarm: three short comm bursts
   o Gestural alarm: extend arm overhead with clenched fist, bend arm 90 degrees at elbow
   o Percussive alarm: three raps in close succession, armor on armor by knocking forearms together

5. If your armor's electronics still function, initiate emergency contaminant flush and antibiotic injections.

6. Resume your mission. Upon your return to base, report directly to quarantine for examination by the base's medical droids.

deployed to volcanic mines where the collection of rare ores is threatened by Rebel guerillas. The armor of a lavatrooper is reinforced with Duravlex to withstand extreme temperatures of up to 1,900 degrees centigrade. Magma stormtroopers are armed with heavy blasters and SS-Mobile-tech flamethrowers.

RADIATION ZONE ASSAULT STORMTROOPERS (RADTROOPERS)

Radiation zone assault troopers, or radtroopers, <u>are deployed in heavy radiation zones,</u> such as those found on inhospitable but strategically valuable planets or battlegrounds scarred by the detonation of fission weapons.

The silver-coated armor of a radtrooper is lined with a lead-polymer that blocks electromagnetic energy. Powered by a backpack unit, it also guards its wearer against outside contaminants by maintaining a breathable, temperature-controlled environment.

Radtroopers carry modified blaster weapons that are unaffected by radiation surges. Standard equipment also includes handheld sensors to measure the level of background radiation and to determine the potential risk to

Imperial slaves that might be assigned to work in the area.

RIOT STORMTROOPERS

The insidious influence of the Rebel Alliance has spread corruption even within loyalist populations. When civil unrest is detected, riot stormtroopers step in to reestablish Imperial order. They are deployed almost exclusively on megalopolis worlds throughout the Core and Colonies—the disobedient worlds that require parental discipline.

Riot stormtroopers are trained at the same Yinchorr academy as the Emperor's Royal Guards. They are unmatched in personal combat and in the use of staff weapons such as the stun baton. They prefer direct combat and do not fear becoming overwhelmed by crowds.

RIOT STORMTROOPER

DURING THE FIGHTING ON IMMALIA, WE RETREATED WHEN A SQUAD OF APPROACHING RADTROOPERS WAS SPOTTED. WE ASSUMED WE WERE OPERATING IN A CONTAMINATED ZONE. TURNED OUT THE EMPIRE JUST HAPPENED TO HAVE RADTROOPER ARMOR AVAILABLE THAT DAY, AND WE GAVE UP THAT GROUND FOR NOTHING. —REEKLAN

DESERT STORMTROOPERS (SANDTROOPERS)

Sandtroopers are stationed on hot, dry worlds where storms of sand, ash, or other particulates can clog breathing filters and jam machinery. A sandtrooper's armor features an advanced filter-flush system for steady breathing, plus cooling recirculators and polarized helmet lenses to eliminate dune glare. Their SD-48 survival backpacks permit them to complete extended missions in unrelenting heat. Each backpack contains several liters of purified water, a miniaturized vaporator for condensing drinking water from the atmosphere, a long-range comlink, and a collapsible reflective shelter.

DESERT STORMTROOPER

IMPERIAL JUMPTROOPERS (SKYTROOPERS)

The colorful heritage of the skytroopers encompasses the rocket-jumpers of the Late Manderon period, the airborne clone troopers of the Clone Wars, and even the infamous jetpack warriors of Mandalore. Like those who came before them, Imperial jumptroopers are experts in air-to-ground attack. Each jumptrooper wears an AJP-400 Hush-About jetpack modified for up to two minutes of continuous operation.

Jumptroopers don't remain airborne for sustained battles. Instead they use their jetpacks to reconnoiter battlefields, reach inaccessible areas, land undetected behind enemy lines, or gain elevation to fire on enemies. They carry heavy plasma disruptors and employ a variety of projectile weapons including rocket launchers, explosive rail charges, and anti-infantry fléchette canisters.

COLD ASSAULT STORMTROOPERS (SNOWTROOPERS)

Like their name suggests, snowtroopers are trained for operation in arctic environments. Their insulated armor features an arctic-camouflage white body glove as an additional layer of thermal protection. Manual controls for regulating the suit's internal systems are located on the breastplate. The lenses of the snowtrooper helmet act as polarized snow goggles, while the faceplate is covered with a breather hood to recirculate air for warmth and prevent ice from forming in the helmet's atmospheric filter. Each snowtrooper carries a survival kit containing a portable heater, a collapsible shelter, spare power packs, a homing beacon, a comm unit, and ion flares.

COLD ASSAULT STORMTROOPER

WETLAND ASSAULT STORMTROOPERS (SWAMPTROOPERS)

The lightweight armor of Imperial swamptroopers is tinted green for camouflage in forested wetlands. These battle theaters are frequently found near lakes, rivers, and other waterways where settlements tend to cluster on habitable planets. Their modified armor incorporates environmental sealants to keep out the many biological perils that thrive in swamps (colonies of toxic bacteria, swarms of stinging insects, amphibious carnivores, and more).

Swamptrooper helmets are fitted with rebreathers to filter breathable oxygen and allow them to operate underwater for a limited time. The lenses of the helmet feature multi-spectrum viewfinders and terrain-mapping software. Swamptroopers carry heavy repeating blasters, and their survival kit includes an emergency float and a serrated vibroknife.

ZERO-G ASSAULT STORMTROOPERS (SPACETROOPERS)

Widely considered the best soldiers in the galaxy, Imperial spacetroopers specialize in assaulting and capturing enemy starships. Like the Imperial Marines, they serve aboard the vessels of the Imperial Navy. Unlike the Marines, spacetroopers operate best in the airless interstellar void.

Spacetrooper armor comes in several configurations, but all models incorporate vacuum sealing and safeguards against hyperspatial radiation. The armor also includes a propulsion system and a small arsenal of anti-starship weaponry. While spacetrooper assault armor is oppressively bulky within standard gravities, it excels when a spacetrooper is launched from a Gamma-class assault shuttle. Essentially, a Zero-G Assault Stormtrooper is a small, single-pilot spacecraft.

Several weapons are incorporated into spacetrooper armor. Laser torches for cutting into the hull of a target vessel are located on the upper forearms. The right gauntlet features a blaster cannon while the left boasts a proton torpedo launcher. Two shoulder-mounted grenade launchers can be used to release gas or smoke grenades after gaining access to the ship's interior.

SCOUT TROOPERS (BIKER SCOUTS)

Imperial scout troopers, or biker scouts, are experts in mobile reconnaissance, trained infiltrators, and survivalists. Equipped with 74-Z speeder bikes, they lead patrols to determine the strength of enemy forces or perform hit-and-fade attacks in support of a larger ground force.

Scout trooper armor is lightweight to allow for a full range of movement. Their helmets incorporate macrobinocular scopes and terrain-following tactical readouts. They carry holdout blaster pistols as well as collapsible E-11 blaster rifles outfitted with sniper scopes, which allow them to eliminate targets from a distance.

A scout trooper field kit contains rations, a reel of micro-cord with a grappling hook, a shielded comlink, a camouflaged shelter, a water purification kit, flares, and an R-4 recon droid.

This is more accurate than I'd like. A single spacetrooper can breach and seize control of a blockade runner. We need countermeasures. We need training. —Leia

Starfighter escorts, for one. Spacetrooper weapons aren't suitable for dogfights. If they get caught in a starfighter's crosshairs, it's all over. —Wedge

EMP bursts are sometimes effective at disrupting the electronic systems of spacetrooper armor. Without power, a spacetrooper can't move. —MADINE

EXCERPT FROM THE IMPERIAL STORMTROOPER CORPS FIELD MANUAL

SECTION 27.B.ST2

SCOUT TROOPERS—RECONNAISSANCE AND SECURING RALLY POINTS

During recon missions maintain comm silence when contact
with the enemy is likely. Minimize travel noise and do not
activate any external lighting sources. When infiltrat-
ing, only move between concealed positions. Select your
next point of concealment and move quickly between locations. If there is reason to believe you are under enemy
observation, remain low to the ground and move in a zigzag
pattern.

Scout troopers are the eyes and ears of the Stormtrooper
Corps. During travel, scouts should check their surroundings for indicators of enemy presence. Such indicators may
include:

◊ Recently disturbed underbrush.

◊ Unnaturally straight lines and angles. This
  may indicate buried machinery or battle droids
  in cover.

◊ Vegetation that appears out of place with its
  surroundings or is of a type not typically
  found on the planet. This is a potential sign
  of enemy camouflage.

◊ Abandoned equipment. Such items could be left
  by a retreating enemy and could provide clues
  to their composition and proximity.

ELITE STORMTROOPER UNITS

THE EMPEROR'S ROYAL GUARD

Charged with the personal protection of His Imperial Majesty, the Royal Guard is the most important unit within the Imperial Military. Candidates for the ranks of the Royal Guard are hand-picked from the academies and from within the ranks of the Stormtrooper Corps. They are trained in combat techniques as well as the art of Echani, unarmed combat at the Imperial Royal Guard Academy on Yinchorr. They practice against one another inside the Squall arena. Their final test, held under the Emperor's watchful gaze, is a battle to the death. The survivor joins the Royal Guard.

Beneath their crimson robes, Royal Guards wear battle armor inspired by the legendary Sun Guards of Thyrsus and wield bladed force pikes. It is said that no Royal Guardsman has ever died in battle against an enemy.

Now that's got to be a lie. —Han

NOVATROOPERS

Stormtroopers who have been selected for a place in the Emperor's honor guard are recognized as Novatroopers. Their armor glistens with the ceremonial colors of black and gold. Novatroopers are rarely encountered outside of official Imperial

Somebody's got to be the best of the best. Luckily I've heard there's only a few dozen of these guys. —Wedge

ceremonies, such as the semi-annual awarding of the Medal of Valor and the Emperor's public address to the citizens of Coruscant at the start of New Year's Fete Week.

CORUSCANT GUARD

The Coruscant Guard maintains peace on the Imperial capital, safeguarding its citizens and ensuring the stability of the world our Emperor calls home. The Coruscant Guard works in conjunction with the Coruscant police, but their members outrank all local law officers. The Coruscant Guards are tasked with maintaining security within key governmental sites including the Imperial Palace and the Pliada di am Imperium. They also escort high-ranking Imperial senators and moffs.

Their armor is optimized for visibility, flexibility, and one-on-one combat. It features extra padding to absorb the impact of blunt trauma and helmet lenses that allow the trooper to see in complete darkness. Their helmet vocoders double as crowd-address loudspeakers. The members of the Coruscant Guard carry force pikes, taser staves, and riot rifles. They operate a fleet of rapid-deployment airspeeders.

EXCERPT FROM THE IMPERIAL STORMTROOPER CORPS FIELD MANUAL

SECTION 0711.X.STC01

CORUSCANT GUARDSMEN—USING THE FORCE PIKE IN ONE-ON-ONE COMBAT

Performing the Smash-and-Slash maneuver:

1. Swing one leg forward and push off your rear leg, making a forward lunge.
2. At the same time, strike your target using the blunt end of the force pike at your target, maintaining a tight grip.
3. Extend your arm closest to the vibroblade end of the force pike, swinging it across your opponent's body.
4. Return to a ready stance. Assess damage to target and prepare for possible counterattack.

Performing an Offensive Parry maneuver:

1. Keep the force pike close to your body, parallel to the ground and slightly above the waist. Use small movements.
2. Intercept the enemy's weapon with the center of the shaft, absorbing the impact.
3. Immediately rotate your arms and hips, using your body's momentum to redirect the enemy weapon back toward its wielder. Aim for the enemy's neck, as this area is often unarmored and is a vulnerable spot for most humanoid species.
4. Return to ready stance. If the enemy is injured and has ceased attacking, perform a finishing blow (see next section).

YOUR EMPEROR COMMANDS YOU: EXPOSE PURSUE DESTROY THOSE WHO WOULD RESIST US!

THE SOLDIERS UNDER YOUR COMMAND LIVE BY THESE WORDS. SO SHOULD YOU.

IMPERIAL STORM COMMANDOS

Beat the Rebels at their own game. The ability to battle a slippery enemy that avoids open combat was the concept behind the formation of the Imperial Storm Commandos.

Storm commandos are the special forces division of the Stormtrooper Corps. They specialize in countering the insurgency tactics of the Rebel Alliance and putting down insurrections or revolutions near Rebel hotbeds. Storm commandos rely on stealth and place an emphasis on sabotage and assassination.

Storm commando armor is similar to that worn by Imperial scout troopers, but it is matte black (which has earned them the nickname "shadow scouts"). The armor finish features a reflective polymer that scatters light and EM radiation, reducing their sensor profile to almost nothing. The armor also generates a radius of sound-dampening up to a meter. Storm commandos are trained to pilot the TIE Hunter, a shielded TIE variant built to dogfight with the Rebellion's T-65 X-wing fighter.

I formed the storm commandos and led them in their early missions. It was those successes that put us in a position to unleash a biological weapon, the Candorian plague, on Dentaal. We were just following orders. That was the last order I took from the Empire. I defected to the Alliance, but I'll be paying my debt to Dentaal until the day I die. —MADINE

TIE Hunter, developed for Storm Commando combat and planetary insertion

STORMTROOPER SPECIALIZATIONS
(EXPERIMENTAL/CLASSIFIED)

SHADOW STORMTROOPERS (BLACKHOLE STORMTROOPERS)

Not to be confused with shadow scouts, shadow stormtroopers serve Agent Blackhole, the head of Imperial Intelligence, and consequently are sometimes called Blackhole stormtroopers. Their missions are classified, but it is known that shadow stormtroopers receive special training in infiltration and ambush tactics.

Their distinctive black armor resembles standard-issue stormtrooper armor, but the differences are much more than cosmetic. The armor of a shadow stormtrooper is made from a stygian-triprismatic polymer that renders it nearly undetectable to sensors. Shadow stormtroopers are also known to carry personal cloaking devices that warp the light around them for an effect close to invisibility.

TERROR TROOPERS

Created as cyborg experiments conducted by the Imperial Department of Military Research, these rare stormtroopers bear the code name Terror Troopers. They specialize in direct combat with sharpened, durasteel talons on their hands and feet. Their cyborg limbs give them enhanced strength, speed, and agility. Their masks, which bear a resemblance to the long-dead Separatist leader General Grievous, provide augmented respiration for the trooper's organic lungs.

TERROR TROOPERS WILL CONTINUE FIGHTING AFTER THE LOSS OF ONE OR MORE LIMBS.

DARK TROOPERS

By General Rom Mohc

Mohc got his army, and the Alliance took it away from him. All dark troopers were lost in the destruction of the Arc Hammer. Or so we hope. —Mothma

As I am the only one qualified to speak of this new technology, I have been asked to prepare this short summary. Remember how close I am to this project and you will understand why I cannot remove all emotion from my words.

In the Clone Wars, we faced battle droids. I was there. I have fought the Emperor's enemies for decades. I was one of the first Zero-G spacetroopers. And while I recognize that technology marches ever onward, I have grave concerns that the current direction of Imperial military research threatens to abandon personal combat altogether.

My dark troopers are droids, yes, but they bring the art of war back to its core, back to the honor of a duel. These iron warriors bring the enemy down to single combat.

The Phase I dark trooper is a skeletal automaton with a frame composed of durable phrik alloy. One arm ends in a vibroblade, the other arm is welded to a metal shield. Phase I is a pure fighter, relying on the art of swordplay. Yet it is merely a testbed for my fully augmented Phase II model.

The Phase II dark trooper is constructed with a reinforced external casing molded from phrik alloy. Its jump pack allows it to fly for short bursts, while its assault cannon releases a withering spray of missiles and plasma shells. Its ARC caster unleashes a harnessed electrical bolt capable of exploding electronics and boiling organic beings from the inside out.

Building on the previous models, Phase III can also be worn as an exosuit, allowing a human operator to engage in direct combat. It is armed with the Phase II's assault cannon as well as two shoulder-mounted missile racks.

It must be noted that I have not yet completed construction on the Phase III and the other two models are still in test mode. But let me say this. I am a stormtrooper, and when I look at my dark troopers, I see brothers-in-arms.

Consider that—and consider my need for increased funding—the next time you hear reports of a battle station that shatters planets. Where is the honor in such a thing?

MISSION REPORT: Heroism in the Emperor's Service

RECOGNITION: Negastrike platoon, 501st Central Garrison Sector M777, Mid Rim

BACKGROUND: The platoon sergeant had previously distinguished his unit in operations on Balmorra, Lasan, and the Metellos Ring. Prior to this incident, the 501st Imperial Legion received orders to contain Trandoshan violence against Imperial settlers who had received the Emperor's blessing to claim the Doshan colony world as their own.

MISSION REPORT: The 501st secured key flashpoints across the equatorial Doshan landmass. Aboard Imperial transport boats, Negastrike platoon advanced against an entrenched Trandoshan nest near the mouth of the Arakka waterway. Demolishing the enemy fortification with thermal detonators and repeating blasters, the platoon soon found itself under fire from a company of Trandoshan raiders who had taken cover beneath the waterway's algae mats.

Negastrike platoon pinned down the Trandoshan raiders, but they could not make landfall without getting picked off on approach. The platoon sergeant ordered his jumptroopers into the air to fire on the enemy from above and to draw their fire. With the hostiles thus engaged, the platoon sergeant ordered his incinerator troopers to saturate the shoreline with chemical spray. Igniting the chemicals with blaster fire, Negastrike platoon watched as the Arakka's algae mats went up in flames, boiling more than one hundred Trandoshans alive.

OUTCOME: The platoon's actions thwarted the enemy's counterattack and allowed the 501st to carry the day. Darth Vader singled out the sergeant of Negastrike platoon by referring to his actions as "notable"—high praise indeed.

THE TRANDOSHANS ARE NOT OUR ALLIES, AND WE DIDN'T LEARN OF THIS BATTLE UNTIL THE DUST HAD SETTLED. I WISH WE COULD HAVE HELPED. —RIEEKAN

PART V

THE IMPERIAL DOCTRINE

By Grand Moff Wilhuff Tarkin

THE PROJECTION OF POWER: THE EMPIRE'S RIGHT TO RULE

We are living in a grand age, one that will shape galactic civilization for the next thousand years. This achievement will be gained through our faithfulness to ideology.

I, who have helped shape the doctrine that underlies the Emperor's New Order, am uniquely qualified to explain its precepts. You, who as a military commander will carry out the Emperor's will, should understand and obey.

When the Republic perished, the cause was clear: two fatal wounds had festered untreated for centuries. First, the Republic sought the input of all its citizens no matter how petty or imbecilic their concerns. Second, the Republic valued the superficial appearance of peace—it maintained no armies of its own until a civil war thrust the Jedi onto the front lines alongside newly minted clone troopers.

The Republic did not project power internally or externally. In truth, the Republic held no true power at all.

The Republic's democracy was a prop for the lazy. It allowed citizens to diffuse personal responsibility throughout the greater whole, ensuring no one would be held accountable for their personal failings. Debates and committees crippled governance and ground progress to a halt. Emperor Palpatine recognizes that all beings are not equal and that decisions determined by a numerical majority do not make them valid.

The Republic's pacifism was a shield for the weak. War is the natural state of things. Consider the fangs of the rancor, which are honed for survival and used to spill blood. Under Emperor Palpatine's rule, Imperial citizens have the opportunity to test their courage in matters of life and death. Revolutionaries, traitors, and

FOR THE FUTURE!

IMPERIAL ORIENTATION DOCUMENT THX-1138

THE NEW ORDER:
CITIZENSHIP, RESPONSIBILITY, & YOU

LORD VADER IS MORE THAN AN INSPIRATIONAL SYMBOL. HIS ORDERS SUPERSEDE THOSE OF ANY MILITARY OFFICER, WITH THE EXCEPTION OF THE EMPEROR HIMSELF.

Tarkin's writings are as odious as the man himself. —Leia

alien savages who do not bow to our Emperor but seek to challenge our authority will meet a merciless end, their territories absorbed into our dominion. We are an Empire, and we _must_ expand if we are to remain vital.

The Empire sweeps aside false social constructs in favor of a rule that is clear and absolute. The burdens of unnecessary freedoms have been shed, and centralized power is made plain. No one doubts their place in the New Order.

As a commander in the Imperial military, you play a vital role in the projection of Imperial power. This authority is needed both internally—to keep order on the Core Worlds and other holdings—and on the frontier where our forces claim new territory in the Emperor's name.

Conquering planets to strip their ore and enslave their people—this is what expansionism means to the Empire. Thankfully we have begun to roll back their advances. —Mothma

THE TARKIN DOCTRINE:
A BLUEPRINT FOR SUPREMACY

I am not one to seek glory at the expense of my Emperor, though my restructuring plan has become widely known as the "Tarkin Doctrine" through no effort of my own. When I first brought the proposal to the Emperor's attention, I knew with confidence that a man in his position would value the ideas of a similar visionary.

The Tarkin Doctrine is the next stage in the development of the New Order. With three guiding principles, the Empire will at last dismantle the lingering constructs of the Old Republic and inspire discipline through intimidation.

PRINCIPLE I:
TERRITORIAL CONSOLIDATION

The Republic divided the galaxy into thousands of sectors, each with a senator and each purporting to represent trillions of citizens. This system birthed noisy chaos. Yet, like the vestigial Imperial Senate, fragments of this system still remain.

The Imperial Senate will soon be erased, and under the Tarkin Doctrine,

so will the primacy of sector governments. The existing galactic map will be divided into Oversectors, each encompassing dozens or hundreds of smaller sectors. A Grand Moff will command each Oversector and will receive generous military allotments appropriate to his station.

Oversectors will allow the Imperial military to react swiftly and decisively. For too long our enemies have relied on a strategy of raid-and-retreat, secure in the belief that a single hyperjump would place them outside the jurisdiction of the nearest sector patrol. <u>A Grand Moff in charge of an Oversector will not think twice about crossing sector borders</u>, nor will he have any need to consult local politicians concerning the actions of the Empire.

I am the first of the Grand Moffs, having been appointed to the rank by Emperor Palpatine himself. I have assumed control of Oversector Outer, encompassing all Imperial holdings throughout the Outer Rim Territories. This dominion is a vast, unbroken ribbon of territory. My own empire,

Nah, we caught on pretty quick. Stage raids at the border of an Oversector and you'll draw two Grand Moffs into a turf war. —Wedge

NEW TERRITORIAL OVERSECTORS WILL EXPAND MILITARY JURISDICTIONS.

TERRITORIAL OVERSECTORS

8

9

10

11

KORPHIR

12

ORD MANTELL

MANDALORE

DORIN

7

3

6

1

CHANDRILA

ALDERAAN

KASHYYYK

KESSEL

PRAXIS CORUSCANT

HUTT SPACE

TYTHON

4

TOYDARIA

ODIK

5

NAL HUTTA

CORELLIA

2

FONDOR

CHARDAAN

20

16

13

ORD PARDRON

14

17

ENDOR

VOGEL

TATOOINE

19

NABOO

QEIMET

RYLOTH

SULLUST

15

JAVIN

18

BESPIN

HOTH

ORTO PLUTONIA

DAGOBAH

MUSTAFAR

one might say, though I am quick to discourage those who offer such praise. My actions serve His Imperial Majesty.

PRINCIPLE II:
RAPID COMMUNICATION

The HoloNet, which permits face-to-face communication across thousands of light years, is one of the wonders of galactic technology. Therefore it is too valuable to leave in the hands of the public. Under the Tarkin Doctrine, all HoloNet transceivers will be real-located to Imperial sector groups, and the entire network will be reprioritized for the coordination of military forces. Each sector flagship will receive its own transceiver and remain in direct contact with Oversector command, while Oversector command will maintain a direct link with the Imperial High Command on Coruscant. Our enemies, who lack this ability, will operate at a severe disadvantage. Furthermore, far-flung Imperial sectors can no longer run wild from lack of discipline, not with the central authority watching their every move.

PRINCIPLE III:
THE RULE OF FEAR

As a military commander, you know the Imperial armed forces excel at spreading terror. Star Destroyers, AT-ATs, and stormtroopers are more than tools—they are symbols of Imperial strength. This is the idea behind the rule of fear. The *fear* of attack can be just as powerful as the use of force.

Yet may I point out the flaw? Our Imperial armed forces are superior in equipment, training, and numbers. But our enemies already know how to fight soldiers. They know how to engage in conventional naval warfare, and how to destroy armored vehicles during a planetary invasion. These battlefield tactics have existed for millennia.

However, with a weapon only Imperial resources could produce, one with an effect so devastating it defied rational explanation, who could counter such a tactic? This extraordinary deterrent would strike a blow so demoralizing the enemy would never recover. It would become a new symbol, one that exemplified the Empire's invincibility. By wielding such a tool, we would extinguish all hope of resistance.

This is no dream. I have made it my calling to research and produce such a superweapon for the Empire's use. With only a handful of

Who was he kidding? A week after this happened, you could buy bootleg HoloNet transceivers from any hustler on Nar Shaddaa. —Han

superweapons—and whispers fanned by propaganda—citizens will be warned against disobedience. If defiance persists, troublesome populations will be sacrificed as an example.

Once the Tarkin Doctrine takes hold, the Empire's rule will be absolute throughout the galaxy.

RULE BY FEAR IS MEANINGLESS IF YOU CANNOT BACK UP YOUR THREATS. SHOW NO MERCY TO TRAITORS.

THE REBELLION:
A MALIGNANT THREAT TO IMPERIAL ORDER

Implementation of the Tarkin Doctrine is critical, for the Empire is under siege by malcontents and traitors. Foremost among them are the fools who have pledged themselves to the "Alliance to Restore the Republic."

They are a gaggle of traitors and bleating know-nothings—Rebels. They are convinced they can return to a time of idealism that only exists in their hazy memories and limited imaginations. The Republic has been dead for two decades, and in light of the Empire's triumphs, the Republic's failings have never been plainer.

Regrettably, the Rebels cannot go ignored. Across the Empire, their cowardly methods have brought death to soldiers and citizens alike.

The origins of the Rebellion are rooted in the Clone Wars. A political minority calling itself the Delegation of the 2000 tried to force its will on Supreme Chancellor Palpatine. Senators Bail Organa of Alderaan and Mon Mothma of Chandrila, despite holding seats on Palpatine's Loyalist Committee, demanded concessions that would have drained executive power and returned it to their greedy, grasping hands. When their desperate attempt to reassert control failed, the New Order arose.

The Emperor issued arrest warrants for the majority of those who had signed the Petition of the 2000. Organa and Mon Mothma held on to their political careers through outward obedience. Behind the scenes, they masterminded the unification of disparate bands of insurgents into what they termed the Rebel Alliance.

The Rebels are traitors and insurrectionists. By their actions, they have all earned death sentences. It is the existence of the Rebellion that underscores the need for superweapons, and if civilians die in the process, that is as it's meant to be. We cannot expect our hands to stay clean when scouring the galaxy of Rebel scum.

If we hope to inspire more Imperial officers to defect, I'm afraid that Tarkin's delusions will need to be addressed by the Alliance. Most high-ranking Imperials have been indoctrinated by similar stories.

—Mothma

THE REBELLION: ACTIVE THREATS

The Rebels have pieced together a military force and placed it under the command of aging generals. They have troopers, capital ships, ground vehicles, and starfighters. Their recruits are often raw and untested. Their officers are often out of touch and deluded, hoping to relive their Clone Wars triumphs.

PAGE'S COMMANDOS

The Rebels are defined by their reliance on guerilla fighting. Rebel special forces excel at such tactics, and Page's Commandos are the worst of the worst. Committed to sabotage and wanton destruction, the members of Page's Commandos have been prioritized by Imperial Intelligence for capture and interrogation.

UNIT SPECIALTIES: Demolition, kidnapping, terrorism, inspiring widespread planetary insurgency

KEY PERSONNEL: Major Bren Derlin, Lieutenant Judder Page

GOOD TO SEE DERLIN'S NAME ATTACHED TO SOME OF THE MAYHEM HE'S CAUSED. HE'S EARNED THE NOTORIETY. —RIEEKAN

RED SQUADRON

The Rebellion has been building a fast-strike starfighter force for years, and recently received a boon when it acquired the designs for the T-65 X-wing fighter from an unfaithful Incom engineer. Red Squadron is composed of the Rebellion's premier fighter pilots. The unit primarily flies the X-wing but relies on the Koensayr BTL-A4 Y-wing for heavy bombing. Their growing list of successes has prompted Alliance Command to list Red Squadron as a floating unit that can be reassigned at will.

OPERATIONS THEATER: Space

UNIT SPECIALTIES: Starfighter dogfighting, convoy raids, convoy escort missions, planetary strafing and bombing runs, capital ship harassment

KEY PERSONNEL: Commander Arhul Narra, Lieutenant Wedge Antilles

i made the list! i'm honored, in a way. Narra was twice the pilot i'll ever be.
—Wedge

AFTER THE BATTLE OF YAVIN, THE REDS BECAME THE ROGUES. IF THE EMPIRE THOUGHT THEY HAD TROUBLES BACK THEN . . .
—LUKE

HIGH-VALUE TARGETS

The following individuals are wanted by the Empire. Full dossiers available upon request. Those marked "capture" or "termination" have been reported to authorized agents of the Bounty Hunters Guild. If you have information on the whereabouts or activities of any of the following targets, contact Imperial Intelligence and the appropriate Oversector Grand Moff.

MARKED FOR OBSERVATION OR ARREST

ADMIRAL GIAL ACKBAR, MON CALA
Naval commander and tactician;
suspected Rebel collaborator

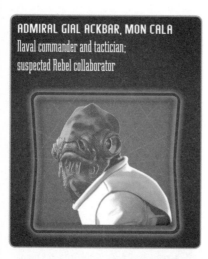

BORSK FEY'LYA, KOTHLIS
High-ranking agent of the Bothan Spynet;
suspected Rebel political advisor

SENATOR BAIL ORGANA, ALDERAAN
Suspected Rebel political advisor

NOTE: His daughter, Leia Organa, holds the current Senate seat from Alderaan and is a suspected provocateur.

I'd like to think I moved up a few rankings in the years since this appeared.
Leia

MARKED FOR CAPTURE OR TERMINATION

SENATOR MON MOTHMA, CHANDRILA
Rebel Commander-in-Chief

[CAPTURE]

GENERAL AIREN CRACKEN, CONTRUUM
Commander of Alliance Intelligence

[TERMINATION]

GENERAL JAN DODONNA, COMMENOR
Commander of Alliance Starfighter Command

[CAPTURE]

SENATOR GARM BEL IBLIS, CORELLIA
Rebel General, may be building a private army

[TERMINATION]

GENERAL CARLIST RIEEKAN, ALDERAAN
Rebel military commander

[TERMINATION]

Fifth billing, behind Bel Iblis?
You're slipping, old friend. —MADINE

SUPERWEAPONS

By Bevel Lemelisk, Imperial Department of Military Research (IDMR)

Limitless military strength packed into a single, destructive machine. It is no fantasy. For millennia, concentrated firepower has been sought by warlords and kings. Here at the IDMR, we have discovered new means to harness the power of enormous kyber crystals only spoken of in legend. We are hard at work crafting the next generation of superweapons in the service of Emperor Palpatine.

WHAT IS A SUPERWEAPON?

An excellent question! "Superweapon" is an inexact term, but generally it describes any weapon that has a destructive capacity far outstripping anything else on the field of battle. During Coruscant's murky proto-history, a Zhell cinderstaff might have passed for a superweapon. In modern times, we have the ability to shatter Coruscant itself. But I'm getting ahead of myself.

DID SUPERWEAPONS EXIST BEFORE THE EMPIRE?

Oh, indeed! I must say, however, that the IDMR has raised the science of superweapons to a rare art.

You need only look up records concerning the Star Forge of the Rakata to read of a historical superweapon. This space station produced unlimited war materiel day and night, never ceasing. Or perform a search on the Shawken Device. This primitive construct would ignite the universe into a conflagration or collapse it into a singularity, depending on which genre of holothriller you prefer. Other stories tell of weapons of immense scale, activated during the ancient battles between Sith and Jedi.

Here are two of my favorite examples. You can see why the IDMR is inspired to outdo the monuments of our ancestors.

SHOCK DRUM

The Sith Empire built this device more than three millennia in the past, taking advantage of a period of détente in its war against the Republic. When placed on the surface of a planet, the Shock Drum emitted concentric ultrasonic waves. Over the course of hours or days, these waves grew in strength until they shook continents. Though never tested, a Shock Drum left unattended would in theory tear a planet apart.

ACTIVE WEAPON: Ultrasonic resonator

HISTORICAL DESTRUCTIVE OUTPUT: Disabling of electronics and weakening of structural supports within a slowly expanding radius; further destructive capacity unverified

MASS SHADOW GENERATOR

Here is a clever conceit—exploiting the quirks of hyperspatial physics! If the surviving documentation is correct, the reactor that powered the Mass Shadow Generator existed in realspace and hyperspace simultaneously. This allowed it to tap the latent energy of a planet's mass shadow and release it as a dangerous gravity wave. Records say that the Republic installed the Mass Shadow Generator at Malachor V near the end of the Mandalorian Wars. Did it work? There's no Malachor V anymore, so it certainly did *something*.

ACTIVE WEAPON: Hyperspatial gravitic generator

HISTORICAL DESTRUCTIVE OUTPUT: Annihilation of capital ships and space stations; unverified destruction of planetary core

INVESTIGATE MALACHOR FOR POSSIBLE SITH OR JEDI ARTIFACTS? —LUKE

WHAT SUPERWEAPONS DOES THE EMPIRE CURRENTLY HAVE AT ITS DISPOSAL?

More than you think! I will detail some below, but understand that even with your level of security clearance, many active projects must remain classified.

TORPEDO SPHERE

A torpedo sphere is an orbital siege platform approximately 1,900 km in diameter. Each is equipped with 125 separate clusters of proton torpedo tubes. By firing proton torpedoes in rapid succession, a torpedo sphere can lay waste to surface targets and capital ships. The Empire has put hundreds of torpedo spheres into production over the last few years, so if you haven't seen one yet you will soon.

ACTIVE WEAPON: Proton torpedoes

DESTRUCTIVE OUTPUT: Concentrated, consecutive damage caused by repeated torpedo impacts within a small radius; can destroy a capital ship or firebomb a large city

VISUAL ELECTROMAGNETIC INTENSIFIER

Not as many VEIs have made it into service as I'd like, and for that I blame myself. The deployment of VEIs is

Too many of these remain in Imperial hands. As we capture more territory, I fear Imperial commanders will stubbornly hold their homeworlds using these miniature Death Stars as fortresses. —Leia

if the Alliance needs a Death Star removed, i think we've got a couple people here who can do that. —Wedge

145

both difficult and time-consuming. This weapon is a network of satellites in stable, synchronous orbit above a target planet. It amplifies light, causing blinding and burning effects on the surface population. Boil the seas? With the VEI it's never been easier!

ACTIVE WEAPON: Amplified electromagnetic radiation

DESTRUCTIVE OUTPUT: Increased temperature, catastrophic flooding, droughts, firestorms, more

ORBITAL NIGHTCLOAK

Recently the IDMR tweaked the Visual Electromagnetic Intensifier and relaunched it as a fresh new brand: the Orbital Nightcloak. This weapon deploys as a satellite network in the same fashion as the VEI, but it performs the opposite function. The Orbital Nightcloak intercepts visual light and other EM wavelengths, plunging a planet into a night that never ends . . . until you decide it can. While it's true that the destruction of a single satellite will short out the entire network, is that not why there is a Navy? To keep the satellites safe? The IDMR can't do everything.

ACTIVE WEAPON: Interception of electromagnetic radiation

DESTRUCTIVE OUTPUT: Decreased temperature, catastrophic ice buildup, mass agricultural die-off, planetary famine, more

WHAT SUPERWEAPONS CAN WE EXPECT FROM THE IDMR IN THE NEAR FUTURE?

How I wish I could answer that question to the full extent of my expertise! Suffice it to say that researchers are sequestered at testing facilities and think tanks across the Empire, tucked away from prying eyes and Rebel sabotage. The projects listed below are experimental and not yet ready for deployment. I hope they give you a taste of the bright glories to come.

SUPERLASER STAR DESTROYER

The Star Destroyer is the backbone of the Imperial Navy. Through retrofitting, we have learned how to make a superlaser the backbone of a Star Destroyer! Such a weapon would allow a Star Destroyer to break apart a small moon, or crack a continent in half. Testing has begun on the *Conqueror*, with more to come as soon as we solve issues of miniaturization and power output.

ACTIVE WEAPON: Superlaser generator and focusing dish

Fatal flaw, there. The Rogues have taken down an entire cloak with one X-wing and a single proton torpedo. —Wedge

Confirmed destroyed at Mostafar. —MADINE

You don't even need to call in a starfighter raid. A commando armed with a targeting missile can lock on and destroy a satellite from the planet's surface. —MADINE

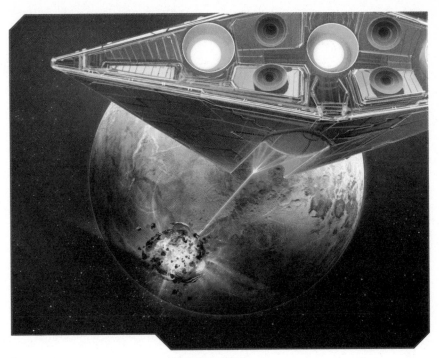

SHIP-MOUNTED SUPERLASERS SHOW PROMISE AT CITY MELTING.

ANTICIPATED DESTRUCTIVE OUTPUT:
Annihilation of a small moon (less than 200 km in diameter)

METAL CRYSTAL PHASE SHIFTER

I'm quite fond of the MCPS, though I recognize we will need to rename it before it is put into active service. In early testing, the MCPS projects an energy field that weakens the molecular bonds of a target. A section of durasteel bathed in an MCPS field will quickly be riddled by thousands of imperceptible cracks. If this should happen to the pressurized hull of a warship, such flaws would trigger a catastrophic loss of structural integrity and sudden venting of the ship's atmosphere into space.

ACTIVE WEAPON: Classified MCPS molecular reconfiguration field

ANTICIPATED DESTRUCTIVE OUTPUT: Capital ships and smaller starships (destroyed indirectly through hull weakening)

NOTE: All superweapons listed here as experimental or planned are to be forwarded to Admiral Drayton in Intelligence. —Mothma

OMEGA FROST

TaggeCo, a nationalized Imperial corporation, has contributed some encouraging developments for a project dubbed Omega Frost. This weapon uses two conductor towers to project an energy field across thousands of kilometers. Within this field, moisture is instantly flash-frozen and molecules have minimal vibration as they approach absolute zero.

ACTIVE WEAPON: Freeze ray

ANTICIPATED DESTRUCTIVE OUTPUT: Shattering most vehicles and structures, instant death for any biological beings

WORLD DEVASTATOR

Now there's a name COMPNOR will love! My colleague Dr. Leth has allowed me to reveal only the most basic information concerning this promising line of research. World Devastators are battlewagons that hover above a planetary surface on anti-gravity repulsors. They project a powerful tractor beam from their ventral bay and draw ground-level detritus into their bellies where it is smelted into raw ores. Internal factories then churn out automated attack fighters to provide the World Devastators with a defensive escort screen.

ACTIVE WEAPON: Overpowered tractor beam and rapid production of attack assets

ANTICIPATED DESTRUCTIVE OUTPUT: Prolonged, sustained damage to planetary infrastructure

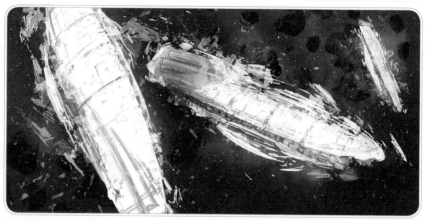

SYSTEMS FROZEN AND HULLS SHEATHED IN ICE, THESE SHIPS HAVE BECOME VICTIMS OF THE OMEGA FROST.

IMPERIAL DS-1 ORBITAL BATTLE STATION: THE DEATH STAR

Again, I have been permitted to share only the essentials of the IDMR's crowning achievement. The DS-1 is the cornerstone of the Imperial "projection of power" doctrine, and those who understand the principle of rule by fear will appreciate the name by which the DS-1 is to be referred in low-security communiqués likely to be intercepted by Bothan Spynet (and from there, make their way into the hands of the Rebels). That name is the Death Star.

The Death Star is the culmination of over two decades of military research. It began as the Weapon, a project hatched by the Geonosian hives during the Clone Wars and intended for use against the Republic by the Separatists. That design was merged with the plans for the Expeditionary Battle Planetoid (co-developed by starship designer Raith Sienar and our very own Grand Moff Tarkin). The result is the DS-1.

Construction of this metal moon has been one of the great achievements of the Imperial age. The Death Star, conceived by geniuses, was built upon the sturdy backs of conscripted Wookiee laborers. At last the Death Star is complete, and Imperial commanders are now free to marvel at its polish and power.

Will more Death Stars follow? Only time will tell, but at the IDMR we have explored two scenarios. Under the first, factory worlds will switch their output to the production of assembly-line duplicates of the current DS-1 design. Under the second, the Empire would build an even larger and more dangerous Death Star, one that would be 160 km in diameter.

I am confident that this is only the beginning. I have spent a lifetime in the field of weapons research, and no client ever settles for a single "ultimate weapon."

Note: If questioned by a non-Imperial news outlet concerning the DS-1 battle station or Death Star, please use its official title: Imperial Planetary Ore Extractor. As a precaution, report the questioner to the Imperial Security Bureau for a thorough follow-up.

OVERALL CONFIGURATION

» 120 km in diameter
» Two polar hemispheres, 12 radial zones
» 1-km wide equatorial trench
» Quadanium steel hull
» Sufficient power, supplies, and consumables for 3 years of continuous operation

PERSONNEL

» 343,000 Naval crewers
» 27,000 Naval officers
» 57,300 gunners
» 285,700 maintenance and support staff
» 167,200 pilots (starfighter, shuttle, tug, and other)
» 42,800 starship support staff
» 607,400 Army troops
» 26,000 stormtroopers
» 400,000 droids
» 843,000 passengers (estimated)

COMPOSITE BEAM SUPERLASER
(FIGURE LABEL 1)

» Position: Northern hemisphere
» 8 particle accelerator tubes project individual beams that converge above a focusing dish to form a single superlaser beam

» Power output: Variable. Settings range from capital ships to planets. Approximate superlaser recharge times range from 1 hour to 24 hours.
» Range: 47,060,000 km

SECONDARY WEAPONS SYSTEMS
(FIGURE LABEL 2)

» 15,000 Taim & Bak D6 turbolaser batteries
» 5,000 Taim & Bak XX-9 heavy turbolasers
» 2,500 SB-920 laser cannons
» 2,500 Borstel Galactic Defense MS-1 ion cannons
» 1,400 SB-920 laser cannons
» 768 Phylon tractor beam generators
» 440 Proton torpedo banks

REACTOR
(FIGURE LABEL 3)

» Sienar Fleet Systems SFS-CR27200 hypermatter reactor
» Thermal exhaust port vents hypermatter reactor wastes

THESE PORTS LED DIRECTLY BACK TO THE REACTOR. INSTANT OVERLOAD. —LUKE

They would have fixed it with the second Death Star, but we showed up before they could finish. —Wedge

Build something around hypermatter, don't be surprised when it blows up. —Han

150

CITY SPRAWLS
(FIGURE LABEL 4)

The DS-1 interior is divided into 84 internal levels, with 257 sublevels each. The station's habitable zones are arranged in self-contained, city-sized units replicated in near-identical configurations. Common features include:

» Armories
» Detention blocks
» Waste compression
» Stormtrooper barracks
» Conference rooms
» TIE fighter hangars (72 TIEs mounted in ceiling racks)
» Shuttle landing bays (atmospheric containment by magnetic field)

STARSHIP AND VEHICLE COMPLEMENT
(FIGURE LABEL 5)

» 7,000 TIE starfighters
» 4 strike cruisers
» 3,600 assault shuttles
» 1,860 dropships
» 1,400 AT-AT walkers
» 1,400 AT-ST scout walkers

Even with all these, the Death Star never launched more than a couple squadrons against us. Lucky for us. —Wedge

HYPERSPACE AND SUBLIGHT ENGINES
(FIGURE LABEL 6)

» Two Sepma 30-5 sublight engines (max sublight speed of 10 MGLT)
» Class 4.0 hyperdrive containing 123 Isu-Sim SSP06 interlinked hyperdrive generators
» Class 20.0 backup hyperdrive

OVERBRIDGE
(FIGURE LABEL 7)

This shielded war room is located above the superlaser focusing dish. From here, the executive command can oversee operations of the Death Star, supervise the battle stations attached to the Imperial Army, Navy, and Stormtrooper Corps, as well as have access to tactical holograms and a secure communications booth.

I was on the Overbridge to witness the deaths of two billion Alderaanians. Everyone else in that room soon followed them into death, and for that I'm grateful. —Leia

THRONE ROOM
(FIGURE LABEL 8)

Located atop a 100-meter tower near the northern pole, this room provides full amenities for His Imperial Majesty, including a private turbolift and throne with command controls. Access to this room is granted to the Emperor, his advisors, and his Royal Guard.

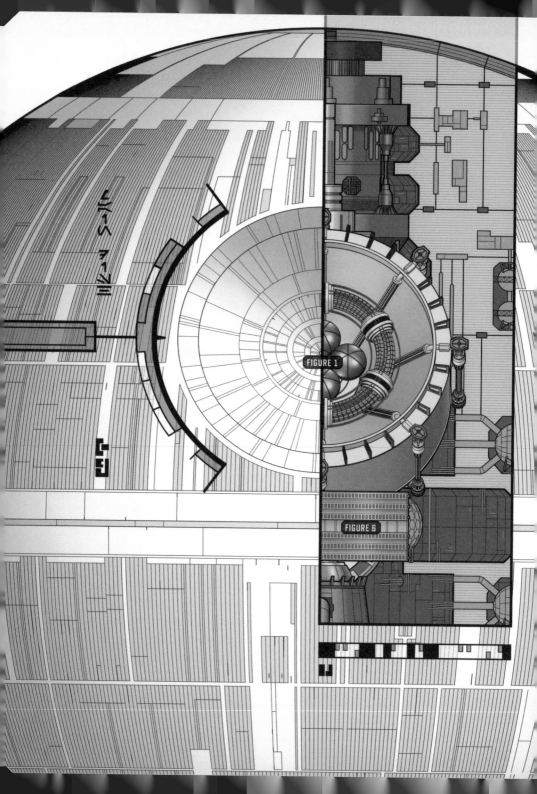

FIGURE 1

FIGURE 6

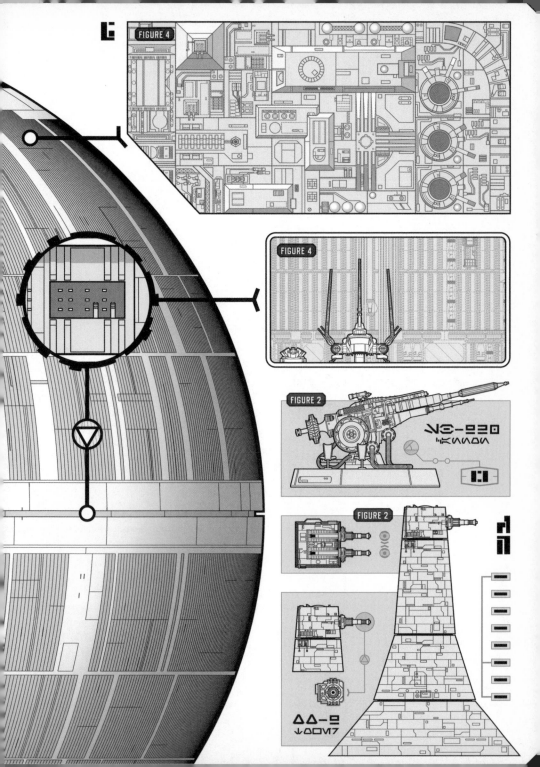

FIGURE 4

FIGURE 4

FIGURE 2

FIGURE 2

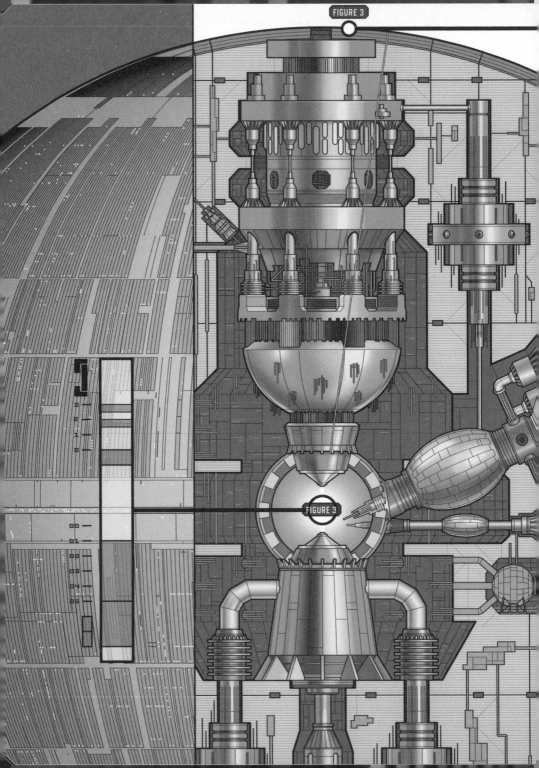

FIGURE 3

FIGURE 3

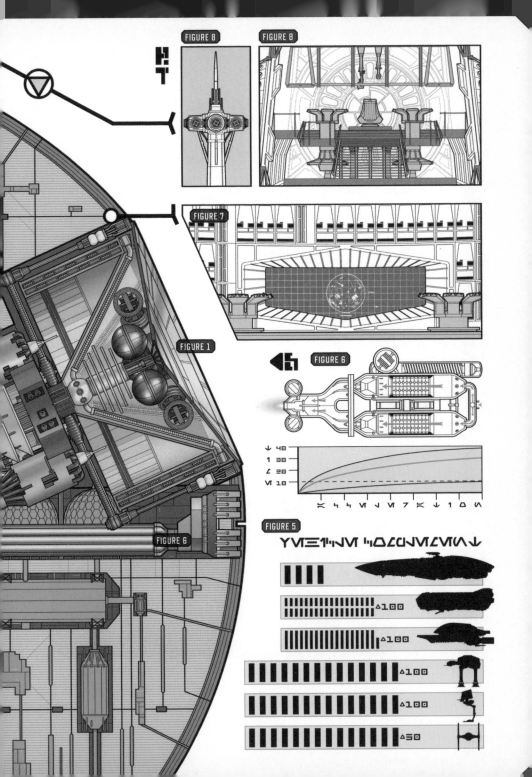

FIGURE 8

FIGURE 8

FIGURE 7

FIGURE 1

FIGURE 6

FIGURE 6

FIGURE 5

PRIORITY TARGETS

WARNING: Activation of the superlaser represents a tremendous expense to the Imperial
military as well as the loss of a potential strategic resource in a habitable or
a resource-rich planet. The following list
of priority targets are grouped according
to the potential damage inflicted on enemy
resources.

OBTAIN A FULL AND CURRENT IMPERIAL
INTELLIGENCE REPORT ON ANY TARGET
BEFORE ACTIVATING DS-1 SUPERLASER.

ONLY PERSONNEL WITH OVERSECTOR
ADMINISTRATIVE RANK AND CURRENT FIRING
CODES PROVIDED BY THE OFFICE OF THE
EMPEROR MAY ACTIVATE DS-1 SUPERLASER.

DO NOT TARGET ANY LISTED WORLD WITHOUT
THE EXPLICIT AUTHORIZATION OF IMPERIAL
HIGH COMMAND AND HIS IMPERIAL MAJESTY.

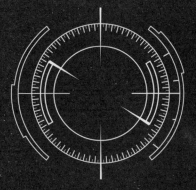

POTENTIAL REBEL BASES, STAGING AREAS, OR DEPOTS (UNCONFIRMED)

- Brigia
- Dantooine
- Edan II
- Golrath
- Polis Massa
- Talay
- Tierfon
- Tomark
- Vergesso

WORLDS PROVIDING POLITICAL OR STRATEGIC AID TO THE REBELLION

- Alderaan
- Chandrila
- Isis
- Kashyyyk
- Mon Cala
- New Plympto
- Ord Pardron
- Ralltiir
- Sullust

A Concluding Note from His Imperial Majesty

You now have vital knowledge of the Empire's armed forces. But this volume is the smallest part of your lesson.

You are a commander. In this role you must excel. To excel you must fight, and when you fight you may die.

Yet even in death you will never be defeated. For the Empire, held aloft on the shoulders of its warriors, is ever victorious. The Imperial Navy, Imperial Army, and the Stormtrooper Corps will fight on after you have fallen.

Through your service, we vanquish our enemies. Through the staggering power of our superweapons, we ensure that our beaten foes stay cowed.

There is no greater calling than to wear the uniform of the Imperial military. Go forth, and enact my will.

Emperor Palpatine

Library of Congress Cataloging-in-Publication Data available.

ISBN: 978-1-4521-4528-0

Imperial Handbook: A Commander's Guide is produced by becker&mayer! LLC

11120 NE 33rd Place, Suite 101
Bellevue, Washington 98004
www.beckermayer.com

Edited by Delia Greve
Designed by Rosanna Villarta Brockley
Production coordination by Jennifer Marx

Lucasfilm Ltd.
Executive Editor: J.W. Rinzler
Art Director: Troy Alders
Keeper of the Holocron: Leland Chee

www.starwars.com

Manufactured in China

MIX
Paper from
responsible sources
FSC® C005748

Text and annotations written by Daniel Wallace

Illustrations by: Chris Trevas and Chris Reiff: Pages 105–108, 152–155; Joe Corroney: Pages 41, 43, 45, 46, 48, 50–52, 80–85, 142, 143; John Van Fleet: Pages 67, 70, 71, 74, 77; Maciej Rebisz: Pages 15, 22, 35, 55, 147, 148; Russell Walks: Pages 4, 10, 126, 135, 139; Velvet Engine Studio: Pages 6, 16, 19, 24, 30, 31, 49, 53, 59, 62, 64, 73, 86, 92, 93, 94, 97, 98, 102, 103, 112, 114–121, 125, 127, 128, 131, 132, 142, 143, 158

10 9 8 7 6 5 4 3 2 1

Chronicle Books LLC
680 Second Street
San Francisco, California 94107

www.chroniclebooks.com